SEAGLASS

SEAGLASS

Eloise Williams

Firefly

First published in 2018
by Firefly Press
25 Gabalfa Road, Llandaff North, Cardiff, CF14 2JJ
www.fireflypress.co.uk

ISBN 9781910080801
ebook ISBN 9781910080818

This book has been published with the support of the Welsh Books Council.

Typeset by Elaine Sharples

Chapter heading artwork by Guy Manning

The poem 'Cofio' by Waldo Williams is reproduced by kind permission
from Eluned Richards (for the estate of Waldo Williams). The translation
of 'Cofio', Waldo Williams, is reproduced here by kind permission of
Alan Llwyd and Cyhoeddiadau Barddas (Barddas Publications). The
translation first appeared in *Stori Waldo Williams: Bardd Heddwch/The
Story of Waldo Williams: Poet of Peace* (2010).

Printed and bound by: PulsioPrint

Dad, who has held my hand through many storms.

Guy, who saved me from drowning.

Prologue

'Kill the witch. Kill the witch.'

The girl is surrounded by snarling faces; an army of enemies baying for blood. A boy becomes a fighter pilot and shoots a round of bullets with his thumbs. For him it's just a game. She can't break through the barricade of linked arms and legs, a circle of *them against us.*

She won't cry. Her throat is harsh, hot, but she won't give them that. She picks up a stone and hurls it blindly. It hits a girl and the crowd breaks in slow motion. She takes her chance and escapes, running hard. Her feet pound fast against the earth, her heart pounds painfully against her chest, the pain in her temple pounding, pounding. She races through the clearing towards home.

They are soon at her heels. Rabid dogs slathering and howling.

'Filthy.'

'Dirty.'

'Disgusting.'

Their hateful cries are caught up by the wind and chase her through the trees.

She's getting closer to her home, deep in the woods, but the pack is getting closer to her. She can't outrun them. She's too young. They're too fast.

Desperate, she crouches inside the hollow of a tree. Holds her breath, scrunches her eyes tight shut.

They find her. She stares into a sea of rage. This is what war is. 'You've had it now, you filthy little...'

She doesn't let them finish. She uncurls, stands up straight and raises her hand in the sign of a curse. She is no witch, but she has to make them believe she is.

'Go on then, kill me if you dare, and I will return from the dead and haunt you all.'

Chapter One

My mam is dying. Everyone knows it.

Dad knows it, though he's pretending it's not happening.

Snow, my little sister, knows it. That's why she isn't speaking anymore.

Gwenni, my ex-best friend, knows it.

Sherlock, my dog, knows it.

I know it. No one will talk to me about it. They just say things like:

'Go and do something, Lark. Be good now.'

'Be quiet, Lark. You know you can be good when you try.'

'Mam is sleeping now, Lark…' Pause while they pat my head. 'Keep the noise down, there's a good girl.'

If someone tells me to be good one more time I'm running away. I'm tall for my age so no one would guess I'm thirteen.

I'm also running away if people say 'well done' to me when I haven't done anything. If they hug me for no reason or if they ignore me completely because they don't know what to say. When you add everything up, the likelihood is that I'm running away.

'Oh, for...!' Dad has road rage but is trying his best to curb his bad language. The car jolts as he slams on the brakes.

'Well done.' I'm not sure if Mam is being sarcastic about Dad's driving, or praising him for not swearing. Either way he smiles at her in that gooey, syrupy way. It's absolutely gross.

'Do you have to?' I like to make my feelings known.

We've been on the road for ages. The morning is full of strange landscapes and perishing cold. The heater is blasting to clear the windscreen and now everything smells meaty. My window doesn't open so I can't let out the stink and I'm sure Dad picked the bendiest route. He calls it *the scenic route.* I call it *the sick route.* Mam has given us a carrier bag in case we need to throw up. I pointed out that it has holes in the bottom, which isn't exactly useful. I've held it in front of my mouth and prepared myself a few times, but nothing has come up. Yet.

'How long left?' I ask for the trillionth time. I don't know why I'm bothering. I might as well be wearing an invisibility cloak. I might as well be a ghost.

'Not far now.' Same cheery sing-song answer from Dad every time, which means all other times he was lying.

We are on our way to a 'secluded spot', near where Mam-gu, my mam's mam grew up. Mam-gu doesn't talk about her childhood there, though Mam doesn't know why. Mam wants to visit the place because she is dying. I shouldn't know this, but it's amazing how sound carries when you try really hard to listen.

Sadly we are not going somewhere amazing like the Galapagos Islands or Kenya. We are staying in Wales. Mam's friends and their kids are coming to join us so we can all have a 'jolly holiday' together. The adults are happy, because they all want to be there to support Mam. As per usual no one cares if their kids want to go with them.

Snow's yolk-yellow felt tip rolls off the seat, onto the floor near my feet. Sherlock looks up to see if it's something interesting then, realising we are still in the hunk-of-junk car, curls up again in his tiny footwell bed, his ears pointed and his furry belly going in and out. He hates travelling. I don't blame him.

Cramped and aching, I squirm against the battered leather. I kick Sherlock a bit by accident, it's pretty difficult not to with the lack of space, and I pat him an apology. I bend to pick up Snow's pen and my stomach claws right up to the back of my throat in bubbling egg-scented fingers, but then gurgles back down. I'm disappointed. If I projectile vomited everywhere perhaps I might get some attention.

'How far *actually* is it?'

Dad puts on the radio. It's the news. He snaps it off again.

'Excuse me. I was listening to that.' I thrash about a bit.

Snow has her knees propped up against the back of Mam's chair in a lung-crushing position, a drawing pad against her thighs. She doodles the things we pass, wiping the window clean every now and again so she can see out. Forlorn houses with cobweb curtains, the shadowy blue hills in the distance, the skeletal trees permanently bending away from the brunt of the wind.

She makes the gulls which wheel and arc in the sky into w's and m's with legs and feet. Her tongue sticks out the side of her mouth when she's concentrating. It has ridges along the sides. I know those are caused by not drinking enough so pass her a water bottle.

'Any chance we could turn the heating off before I die of dehydration?'

I gasp, sucking the word 'die' back into my mouth, swallowing it down deep into my guts, so it's lost in my intestines, unable to find its way out.

Dad pulls over. He's going to give me a row. Good. I am one hundred percent ready for a real humdinger. I'm always ready for an argument these days, but I still want to cry afterwards. Every. Single. Time. It's pathetic. I'm not going to cry today though. I've got good reason to be livid today.

This has got to be the worst thirteenth birthday ever.

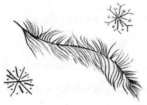

Chapter Two

'What about here?' Dad nods to a shop on the sea front which looks like it hasn't been open since the war.

'What are you hoping to buy with your ration book?' I am the queen of sarcasm.

'I'll have to put my face on,' Mam smiles, but it puts Dad on his guard. 'Chill out, love. I just want to look my best.' She turns and shakes her head at me in mock disbelief. I try my best to smile back.

This is the third shop we've stopped outside. Mam is afraid to go into some of them. She prefers small ones with no other customers when she is feeling ill. Sometimes she gets right to the entrance and then has to turn around. She was told off at one this morning because she froze on the spot which activated the automatic doors. I hope the shop-owner freezes to death after the way he spoke to her and I'm glad I told him so.

I'm sorry about their shocked faces. And I'm sorry that I made that little girl cry because I was shouting, and Dad had to explain that I have 'anger issues'. But no one has a go at my mam and gets away with it. Especially not now.

I look at her profile and try to stamp it on my brain so that I will never forget the details. The bump in her nose, the way her hair curls next to her ear, the wrinkles at the edge of her eyes, the silver droplet earrings that she wears when she wants to look her best. I catch Dad looking in the rear-view mirror at me.

'What?'

'Nothing.'

'Why are you gawping at me then?'

'Lark. Calm down, for goodness' sake.'

'I am calm. Supremely calm. But thanks for the advice.'

Dad looks at Mam and she nods. I think we are the only family in the world who need such an agonising decision-making process over going into a stupid shop.

Sherlock jumps up onto my lap and starts

9

clawing at the door handle to get out, pressing his nose into the steamed-up window. He hates being cooped up even more than I do.

'I'm taking Sherlock for a wee walk.'

Mam nods stiffly, rifling through her shoulder bag.

'Snow, are you coming?' My voice comes out sulky, even though I hadn't intended it.

She's too focused on her drawing to notice that we've stopped. She's really good at art for a kid her age. I'll tell her one day, when I am ready to say something nice again. She's drawn us outside: Sherlock, with tufted ears and a rainbow of arrows above his tail to show it's wagging; Dad, tall, smart and wearing his racing-green wellies; Mam, just an outline so far; me holding a bright purple bird as if I'm coaxing it to fly; and her holding the pen and paper that she's using now. She's used a light brown felt tip to make hers and my skin look right. Dad is a darker brown and she's done Mam in pink. Mam says families come in lots of different colours and it doesn't matter what colour you are. I agree. I glance at Snow's picture again. She's put straight lines for our mouths so none of us are smiling, which is about right too.

'Earth to Snow. Come in, Snow.' I wave my hand in front of her face and she looks up at me and shrugs her shoulders. There are tiny bits of dandruff all over them and speckled in her hair. I'll have to make sure she gets some good shampoo, so the other kids don't pick on her, because then I'll have to punch them, and Dad will be disappointed again, and Mam will be upset again, again, again.

'Snow can come into the shop with me and Dad will come with you.' When Mam says something, nobody argues. She applies some lippy without looking in the mirror then wipes *Paradise Pink* from her front teeth with her finger.

Dad stretches and piano-player cracks his fingers. He smiles at me. 'Bit of sea air will do us all the power of good.'

They've been talking about the *sea air* since we decided to come here. Like it will magic away Mam's illness. Like it will blow through her body and make her fresh again.

'Fine.' Shoving my thumbs through the holes I've made in the cuffs of my favourite red jumper, I open the door, so Sherlock can take a great step for dog-kind. I get out grumpily, slamming the door behind me.

Sherlock lifts his leg against everything and then scampers off, tongue lolling, tail wagging, nose sniffing. Traitor. Mam climbs out of the car carefully but trying not to show it. She's put on her sunglasses, so I can't read her expression. Snow comes out squinting like a mole. She is small for her eight years and much too thin. I cross the lane to get a good look at the sea.

It's cold enough for polar bears. If I saw an iceberg on the horizon I wouldn't bat an eyelid. I wouldn't be able to bat an eyelid because they would be frozen open. Sherlock makes a beeline for the far-off white-horse waves. Apart from him, the beach is empty. Bleached bunting flaps from a lamppost where they probably had a carnival a hundred years ago and a rusted sign reads: 'Beware. Strong tides. Danger of Drowning.' Cheerful stuff.

Because October half term hasn't even started yet there is nobody about. I think that's why Dad chose to come ahead. That's why we got special dispensation to get out of school three days early. So we could slip in here unnoticed and not put any stress on Mam. It wasn't so he could ruin my special day. It was for Mam because she's really ill and I need to stop being selfish.

'Well? What do you think?' Dad comes up behind me and ruffles my hair, which I hate.

I tug it away from my eyes. 'It's practically Arctic here.'

'You take some pleasing, Miss Lark.'

I scowl.

'There's only a tiny chill in the air.'

I double scowl and shiver. I wish I could *cwtch* him like I used to. He has that biscuity aroma because his clothes haven't dried quickly enough. It's one of my favourite smells.

He looks out over the water and breathes deeply like those yoga people do. To be fair, it is pretty. If I was in a better mood, I'd be splashing about with Sherlock by now despite the cold conditions.

'Look, a gannet.' Dad points to a white bird far off, and I watch it plummet headlong through the sky, corkscrewing its wings around its body as it dives, then plunging into the sea so fast I think it will never survive. It surfaces and takes flight and I imagine the water from its wings turning to rainbow diamonds as they fall. This is the kind of thing I used to love when I was the other me. The me I was before.

'It's just a bird.'

'It's a thing of beauty, just like you.'

I move before he ruffles my hair again. I'll cry if he keeps being nice to me.

'Shall I annoy you with some extremely educational facts about the place?'

'If you absolutely have to.' Facts are one of my weak points. I adore a good fact.

'This coast boasts a third of the world's population of Manx Shearwaters.'

'All of the wows.' I'm being difficult. I am the world's biggest animal lover and birds are my favourite.

'The remains of several bomber planes lie on the ocean bed. The *Dead Eye* wreck also languishes at the bottom of the bay.' He does seriously incompetent dead-sailor acting, going sort of cross-eyed but not quite.

'You can stop treating me like I'm stupid now if you like.' I carry on acting super-bored.

'Unexploded bombs have been known to wash up on the beach, so if you discover anything unusual you are asked to call the police immediately.'

'Obviously.'

'The number you should call is…'

'Wait. How do you know all this?'

'Lark, you know your father well enough to understand that he is just incredibly intelligent and knowledgeable on all subjects.'

'Yeah, right.'

'Also, he can read.' He points to a sign I hadn't noticed.

'Funny.'

'I can tell you a few jokes too, if you like?'

'No, thanks. Really. No.'

'That would be a "no" then.'

Sherlock emerges from the sea and shakes himself as if he's in a shampoo commercial. I whistle to him and watch his disgruntled return.

'Not far now, mate.' Dad has said this so many times I have stopped believing we will arrive anywhere at all. Ever. I tut. 'Come on. Before we get frostbite in these "Arctic" conditions.'

Sarcasm runs in the family. All of us are good at it.

Mam and Snow are out of the shop and waiting with our hessian bags full. Snow has the shopping. Mam is fussing, trying to take the bags from her. They look heavy, but Snow isn't giving them up. I love her for her stubbornness. Dad takes them, but Snow keeps a load of old tourist information leaflets, shoving them into her satchel. She's always drawing things from leaflets – castles, flowers, Celtic crosses, forests, churches, graves. I grab one from her.

'The Curse of the Witch Woods.'

'It's just another fabricated story to bring the tourists in.' Dad's expression darkens.

'Childish.' I fling it back at Snow. She has weals on her fingers from the bag handles. I should be able to protect her more.

I should never have told her that Mam was dying. I should have kept it from her, like big sisters are supposed to do. She is only eight and I have already bulldozed through her life with my extra massive gob.

Dad hops back into the driver's seat like it's the best place in the world and studies a map. Snow clambers into the back and starts drawing the bay in an accurate grey. Sherlock pulls at his lead trying not to get back in the car. I pick him up and cuddle him so that he'll know I still love him, even though we are putting him through this torture. Mam tightens the belt of her vintage mac and breathes the sea air in deeply.

'It's going to be good here, Lark. I can feel it in my bones.'

She smiles that too-bright smile and there is a line of *Paradise Pink* between her two front teeth. I don't tell her. A tear slides from behind her sunglasses. I pretend it is caused by the cutting wind. Perhaps she's right. Perhaps the waters here hold healing powers. Perhaps I should be like Snow and believe in magic. It's almost impossible when you're thirteen. I get into the car with Sherlock and we both sulk. The springs in the seat stick into my legs and my cushion is soggy with condensation.

There's a whole new, really weird smell now too. 'Is something on fire?'

Dad is fumbling and cussing a bit in the front. He's burnt his thumb lighting three tea-light candles, which he's put on a Victoria sponge. They turn and hold it towards me, singing 'Happy Birthday' in the out-of-tune way we have perfected over the years. Snow conducts with her fingers instead of singing and Sherlock barks excitedly and tries to jump up to snaffle the cake.

'I'm sorry you've had to be cooped up in here all day.' The lipstick is finally gone. 'But this place is going to be great. A lovely break. For all of us.'

'It's fine. I mean, I wouldn't say it's the best birthday I've ever had but, you know, it's alright. I get it.' And I do. I let go of all the things I hoped my thirteenth birthday would be and try to be an adult.

'Don't forget to make a wish.'

I blow out the candles, then avoid Mam's gaze.

'Not far now, kids. Not far now.' Dad folds the map scruffily and starts the engine. We jerk to a start. I look out at the sea. Maybe I'll go swimming, if I can get hold of a wetsuit. I look at my family. They are not so hopeless, take away the obvious weirdness. Not *completely* hopeless anyway. I glance back at the shop and wish I hadn't.

Two girls stand in the doorway, clearly talking about us. My anger bubbles up straight away. I can't stand it when people say things about me. I'm the only one to notice, so as we pull out, I put up my fingers and give them the sign of a curse I saw once on TV.

So much for it being alright here. I hate it already.

Chapter Three

'Please tell me this is a joke.' I check my phone again. There's still no signal. 'I hate this place with a passion.'

We have turned off the main road – the bit that was actually nice – onto a lane full of warnings about not going to the beach without an adult, as if we are three years old. If I crane my neck, I can just make out the sea in the distance.

'You haven't even got outside the door yet, Lark.'

'You're right.' I get out of the car. 'I still hate it.'

With no signal, I don't know if Gwenni has texted me for my birthday. We aren't ever talking again ever, ever, but it'd be good to know if she's at the grovelling stage. I try to send a text. A bleep, followed by a nothing exclamation mark. I triple hate it here.

The other families that are staying with us will

arrive in a couple of days, and I'll have to see Gwenni whether I like it or not. Dad said we'd be the only people staying at the caravan site, which is a bit weird. I suppose nobody else wants to be out here in October. I can't say I'm surprised, it's so far from anything and will be more than a bit spooky after dark.

I put a brave face on and turn to my sister. She looks ragged with tiredness and completely crumpled. It doesn't help that she has one of my old coats on, the pale blue puffa with the hood. It's far too big for her and now Mam has sewn snowflakes all over it it's even more obviously shabby. Times are hard for everyone nowadays and Mam has tried to upcycle our clothes. We don't want to tell her it hasn't worked. Dad is a mechanic but since he's been laid off we are all trying to do our best.

'Come on, Snow. Let's check out if there's *anything* to do here.'

This holiday with Mam's friends is the stupidest idea anyone ever had. They had this stupidest idea at one of their parties, which explains a lot. I'd rather be on a plane with a passport, going somewhere nice on our own, but I guess Mam wants to make the most of her friends now, so we just have to lump it. Mam-gu suggested we choose this particular site. She still knows people around here and used her connections to rent us all caravans cheaply. Though why anyone would pay much to stay here is beyond me.

A black-backed gull laughs cronkily overhead. Perhaps the wildlife will be interesting at least.

'Come on, this way.' I grab Snow's hand and she comes gratefully. Neither of us wants to help unpack. We stagger to where we can get the best view, our muscles aching from being cramped up for so long. A whistle escapes my mouth. 'Now that actually is pretty good.'

We've picked the best caravan, the one overlooking the small path down to the stream. The others are going to be gutted they didn't arrive first. 'Look at the way the current runs. The reflection makes the sky look like it's wobbling.'

Snow points in the other direction.

'The Forbidden Beach?' The first on Dad's list of warnings on having respect for the sea. 'How do you fancy a bit of cliff climbing?' I'm only half joking. 'And the way the water glitters is just so…'

It hits me suddenly – why we're here, why Mam needs a holiday. I turn away from Snow, so she won't see there's anything wrong. I am always turning away to hide my feelings. I'm a human roundabout.

'I just love these yellow flowers.' I act like I'm engrossed in smelling them, even though they have thorns that could lacerate your nose. 'They smell like coconut in the sun.' In this howling wind they don't smell of anything at all. 'Shall we go along the stream to the sea?'

Of course, I don't expect an answer from Snow, but I can't help asking her questions, hoping she'll say something. Anything. Her voice is locked deep down inside her, like all my happiness is in me.

My left sock falls down inside my jeans. I pull it up and myself together.

Snow has moseyed off in the wrong direction, which is just completely typical. Even though the Forbidden Beach is beckoning me, I have responsibilities and I can't leave her. She has taken to wandering off too many times of late. It can be difficult to find her again since she stopped answering our calls. 'Snow, wait for me.'

The caravan site is nestled in a dip. She is walking into the chirruping woods behind. I follow her, feeling sorry for the poor kid. When you are eight, you never get to be alone. Rule.

It's beautiful in here. The trees have dipped themselves in autumn colours, reds and yellows, russets and rusts, dusky purples and blues further in, the lightest mint fringes behind. I can imagine the owls that hunt in these woods, the falcons and kestrels and kites. I see the peach flash of a nuthatch's belly and know that it will be a bird lover's paradise.

'Let's not go too far in, OK?' I do the big-sister thing. 'Not right now anyway.'

We've all heard the stories of kids who wandered off and ran into bad luck or worse.

'Just in case Mam needs us.' Saying this makes us feel less like cowards.

I can hear Sherlock barking back at the caravan, but he stays with Mam most of the time now.

Snow is just ahead of me, weaving her way through the trees. This is the problem with little sisters. You are always expected to watch out for them, and stand up for them, and give them all the best opportunities and a better place to sleep.

'Ouch!' Something sharp cuts into me through my jeans. Bending down, I see a shard of glass, still attached to a metal window frame. A bead of bright red oozes through my denim. I wipe it, then lick the blood from my fingers. It tastes of copper and pain, and is a way gross thing to do, so I check around that no one saw me.

Only a squirrel, who stares at me then pretends to eat the acorn he's holding. I know he'll be stowing that nut away somewhere for later.

'Snow. Can we go back now please?'

She doesn't answer, naturally.

I decide to quit talking myself, while I pull apart the already broken pane. It feels good to shatter something. I crack it to bits and feel in control for once.

Panting, I start my countdown from ten to get rid of my anger.

Ten, the wind in the trees sounds angry.

Nine, I'm cold and really fed up.

Eight, my sleeves are silver with snot.

Seven, nothing is fair.

Six, seriously, nothing is fair.

Five, there's a hollow in the tree in front of me.

Four, I could squeeze into it and hide from everyone.

Three, it would be nice to disappear for a while.

Two, I need to grow up and stop acting like I'm twelve.

One.

I imagine a girl crouched in a ball in this hollow place, hiding, desperate not to be seen. The girl isn't me. A buzzard whistles high above. I look for Snow.

For a moment I can't see her, then I spot her snowflakes sparkling further into the woods. I think I hear her laugh. I listen hard. Snow hasn't laughed in months. It feels like years.

There is nothing but the *shush* of the branches, the sound of the leaves crackling on the wood floor. I watch her disappearing through the trees ahead. I let her go. I want to see what it feels like to lose someone.

When she is almost out of sight, I bottle it, and run after her as fast as I can. Mam and Dad will be well annoyed if I lose her on Day One.

'Snow!'

She's stopped with her back to me, staring at something.

'What could possibly be interesting here?'

Out of nowhere I'm too hot. I pull the neck of my jumper away from my throat. It feels like it's constricting my airways. An odd burning shivering washes over me, like a fever. The world tilts, there's a jigsaw of sky, the flash of something out there in the woods. Gone, as quickly as it came.

Snow ignores me.

'Why didn't you wait for me? Seriously. You are such a nightmare.'

I sound crosser than I mean to. Snow doesn't react, but keeps staring straight ahead. Unusually, she's smiling. I should be glad but I'm not.

'I said, you could have waited. I'm not your keeper.'

She comes up close to me, scrutinizes me, then presses my cheeks with the pads of her thumbs before squashing my face like I've got stuck in the doors of a lift. It's something we've done since we were kids.

'It's alright. Just hang on for me next time. OK? Can we go now? I feel odd.'

Shaking her head vehemently, Snow points at something hidden through the trees.

It's the ruin of a house. It's pretty well camouflaged, almost completely covered in ivy creepers, dead branches and brambles.

Snow takes the small notebook she always carries with her out of her pocket and writes. Her tongue sticks out at the side. A tiny speckled moth lands on the page right next to her fingers and she stops to let it beat its wings undisturbed. When it flies off, it leaves a delicate trail of wing dust next to her words: '*Owr new den.*'

Chapter Four

I haven't the heart to correct her spelling. She looks so hopeful and shy.

'Yes. It's our new den. And it'll be the best den anyone has ever had. Come on.'

The shivering feeling has gone. I've decided to be benevolent now that I'm thirteen. I will win prizes for my saintly patience. 'Let's investigate.'

It doesn't look like the best den ever, but I feel heroic as I begin planning how to keep the others out when they arrive. We'll use that Witch Woods claptrap to keep the little kids away. We'll have to think of something a bit more effective for the older ones. 'This way.'

We go closer, magnificent explorers crossing uncharted territory. The bricks are completely strangled in green and it takes a good while to find the doorway.

'We should bring a knife and cut the worst of it

down.' There's nothing I like better than hacking things. 'Be careful when you come through here.'

I yank at a jungle of bindweed and am extraordinarily satisfied when lots of it comes down. Holding the worst of the brambles back, I squeeze my way in and Snow follows me into what must have, at one time, been a really small cottage and is now four crumbling walls with a tangled emerald roof.

I become a historian. 'That's where the chimney would have been. You see here, it connects to a fireplace. And the stairs would have been here.'

I run my hand along the jutted bricks, half expecting to be blasted into the past like in one of those dreadful Sunday afternoon films. 'This would have been the main living area because they wouldn't have had any heating anywhere else.'

I'm even putting on one of those voices that TV presenters use in those house programmes I love. It's lucky only Snow is here to see. The other kids would rip me to shreds. Turn to camera. 'The toilet would probably have been outdoors. Quite possibly at the end of the garden.'

Snow loses interest and goes over to the other corner. I'm a bit relieved as I was running out of vaguely historical guesses. I wander about examining the place properly. There's no evidence of anyone else having been here, which is good but also unusual. I know we are in a lonely spot, but most places, however wild, have been invaded by crisp packets and dog-poo bags and other signs of laziness, litter and life.

A burning cold shiver runs the length of my body again and I fold my goose-pimpled arms against it as a wave of sadness washes over me. I have never felt lonelier than at this very second. Something dark flickers at the corner of my eye, but when I focus it's gone.

All that travelling must have made me feel peculiar. I've had very little sleep.

Something brushes the nape of my neck and I spin round. There's nothing there. The wind, of course, or a falling leaf. Get a grip on yourself, Lark, you enormous weirdo. There's nothing to be afraid of in a few crumbling bricks.

'Snow. What are you doing?'

She's crouched down in the corner, scrabbling at something. I hope it's an owl pellet. Then we can pull it apart and see what it's been eating from the bones.

'Snow? What is it?' I feel uneasy, looking at her hunched down there. When I say her name, she looks over her shoulder furtively as if she wants me to go away. 'I said, what is it? Show me.'

Grabbing hold of her shoulder, I pull her back. She's been gouging at the earth with her fingernails. It's a doll. Its head stares up out of the mud. Its painted eyes have rubbed off and it has tiny hairline cracks running through its china face.

'Ew. That's macabre.'

Snow pushes me away and kneels forward to dig it out.

'Do you *really* want that? Seriously?'

She excavates it and gently rubs some of the mud from its face. The body must have been made of a sack or something, but it still has tiny china hands at the ends of its worm-eaten cloth arms. Utterly, totally gross. Snow stares into its cold, dead, empty eyes as if she is in love with it.

'Snow, it's horrible. It looks like it will kill you in your sleep. Honestly. I can get you a better doll.'

She bites her teeth together in that way she has and holds it even tighter.

A crow *cwarak-cwaraks* loudly and flies right next to my head, too close, clipping the edge of my hair. I'm shivering hot again and seriously dizzy. Snow's face goes blurry and the wind picks up and banshees through the cracks in the walls. I don't want to make this our den.

'OK. Keep the doll. See if I care. Do whatever you like.' I push my way through the thorns out into the bristling woods. When I can see our caravan, I calm down enough to check Snow is following. She is, which is a relief. She is carrying the doll, which isn't.

I don't know what it is about that thing, but it really creeps me out.

Chapter Five

I want to go to the sea to clear my head, but I swear that Mam and Dad have some kind of tracking device on us. We try to keep out of their sightline as we head for the water. No chance.

'Lark. Snow. Come here and help your mam unpack.' Honestly, Dad's voice would carry over a football crowd on the brink of a win.

I had hoped to stall for time, before returning to the reek of illness in the caravan, with the walls pressing in. But I must do as I'm told. All. The. Time. At least Snow has got rid of that awful doll, though I don't know where she put it. Out of sight, out of mind. Hopefully.

I don't pretend to be happy about helping. Eventually, after I've scratched a piece of furniture by accident, Mam takes pity on us.

'Go on then. Off you go.'

We burst out, two caged nightingales released to sing our song.

'Come on, Snow. Let's explore. Come on, Sherlock. Good boy.'

We hit the ground running and keep racing until we are far enough away from the caravan that they can't call us back. Panting, we flop down on the bank of the stream. Snow collapses backwards and starts tracing the shapes of clouds with her fingers in a way that I know means she is turning them into art. Sherlock pees on every available thing, then barks to break the silence that clings to the edge of the water.

Snow sits up and looks at me. I understand immediately. It's like that when you've known someone your whole entire life.

'The Forbidden Beach it is.'

She is on her feet in seconds and we break Dad's rules without even bothering to shake on it. With Mam this way and him distracted, we can pretty much do what we like.

'Herons, look.' I point far into the distance. 'They look like pterodactyls, right? And there, that's an egret bobbing its head like a chicken.'

Snow gives me the face to tell me I'm boring her with my bird talk and I take the hint.

We walk the rest of the way cheerfully, me

fighting back the urge to point out the way the water chatters over pebbles or the trampled paths made by animals coming to drink. At the mouth of the stream we stop, and I know that we are both thinking we shouldn't be doing this. Mam and Dad would throw a hissy fit if they knew we were here on our own. They'll calm down when the rest of our lot arrive, as we'll never have a chance to be completely alone then.

'I declare this place No Man's Land.' I indicate the area around the stream. 'This is our side and that is The Others' and as long as we don't pass this middle bit then we will be alright.'

As if to show he doesn't care, Sherlock wades straight out into the middle of the stream and lies in it to cool down. His total disregard for any rules makes us feel better. Snow lies on the sand and starts making an angel by flapping her arms and Sherlock comes out of the water and digs a hole to bury a stone.

The town where those girls were is in one direction, I can see the matchbox-sized houses. There are sand dunes in the other. We are in the throat of the land, its mouth formed by a semicircle of cliffs. Let's hope it doesn't swallow us.

'There's a fog a'coming in.' I do my best impression of a pirate. It isn't good. Add bad acting to the list of things that run in the family. Snow sits up to look at the far-off wisps, dismisses them and goes back to making her angel.

Dad warned us about every possible danger on the way here and about seventeen hours into his warnings, just after quicksand and ticks, he got to 'the dangers of a sea fret'. It doesn't look all that dangerous to me. Just a drifting wall of white a long way off. It's beautiful. Like a cloud that's come down for a drink.

Snow stops her angel, then starts again with a shrug, accidentally putting shoulders on its wings. I laugh and haul myself up. 'Race you.'

I dash headlong for the sea, yanking my boots off at the tide's edge and shoving my socks inside them, only rolling up my jeans once they are already soaked at the hems. 'Argh. It's freezing. Snow, come on, you coward.'

I kick up crystal chandeliers and she tucks the ends of her dress into her pants and paddles out to kick some back. The waves are dead calm now the wind has disappeared, so I don't need to worry about her. Sherlock patrols the shallows, moving his head on a wonk from side to side as if he's trying to make sense of us. It's hilarious. Snow rushes up and tickles his scruff in the way he loves then tiptoes along the sea's lacy edge. I follow, shoving my feet into my boots with sand still all over my toes. My jeans stick to my legs and make them itch but it's worth it for the glorious feeling of freedom. 'Come on. Let's look over here.'

Scanning the beach, I can only see one random dog walker just leaving The Others' side. It's the perfect opportunity to investigate the lie of the land, before Mam's friends arrive and we lose the upper hand.

The fog has wiped out the view of the town, which means it's coming closer. I can't see the cliffs on the one side of the bay anymore. I'm surprised by how much it has grown in such a short time. But I'm not in the mood for warnings and doubts.

'Snow, look.' I pick up a piece of palest mint-green on the beach and hold it up triumphantly.

Snow comes over to look.

'Lorelei had a necklace with one on it, remember?'

Crouching down, Snow writes SEAGLASS in the sand with her finger.

'We can use it to make pictures on your light box.' Snow has a light box to make art, since Mam got ill and she stopped talking. We brought it with us. It's supposed to help her express herself. So far, it's been a waste of time. 'Come on, let's search for other bits.'

It's a brilliant idea, if I say so myself, and I'm thrilled to see Snow excited about searching. We look among the stones and pebbles, finding a wobbly blue piece and the brown lip of a bottle, but it's not enough. The fog is creeping towards us, but we are still alright and it's such a good idea, I can't let it go just yet. Maybe it will make Mam smile. A real smile, not just a lipstick one.

'You carry on here and I'll check over there.' I hop from stone to stone to cross the stream, through No Man's Land.

Snow starts following me immediately. I raise my voice. 'Stay on that side. Why don't you listen for once?'

She pouts, but I just ignore her. She'll be alright for ten minutes. She has Sherlock with her for protection.

Climbing over the first lot of rocks isn't too simple. They are covered in beards of slimy seaweed and I'm trying not to step on the mussel shells and sea snails because they are still alive and deserve a chance like everything else. I hoped I'd find lots of sea glass here, but there are just large rounded pebbles and piles of flotsam and jetsam. If I ever decide to collect rubber gloves, rope, bits of net, broken lighters, cans, fishhooks, straws or plastic bottles, this will be where I'll come. Sherlock barks behind me and I can tell he is unhappy that his pack has split.

I press on. I can't go back with empty pockets. I've decided to make the beach my new best friend. It doesn't talk back to me or give me a hard time about how freaky I am, and it doesn't lose interest in me when it has a new boyfriend called Jake who everyone knows is an absolute idiot. It doesn't borrow my red boots and bring them back with the heels so worn down that I can never wear them again.

Oystercatchers squabble in the distance and the fog is like a shimmering wall of white. It's gathered incredibly quickly and suddenly it's so close I can almost touch it. I imagine what it would feel like to wear it as a cloak. There's something so magical about the way the world has spun it from thin air. If only I could lose myself in it and never come back.

There's no sea glass here. I should go back, but I'm fairly certain I can survive some fog. I check that Snow isn't following. I can just make her out at the very edge of the stream. It makes me feel guilty to see her shoulders slump and hear Sherlock's mournful whine. I can find my way back in three seconds flat. It's hardly like I've abandoned them. I'll only be a minute or two.

Taking on the challenge of another set of rocks, I convince myself that it's fine to leave my little sister alone on a beach where we are not allowed to be in the first place with fog coming in. She'll be OK if I'm really quick. It's not fair that I have to be the carer all the time. Dark thoughts scuttle around my brain like full-bodied spiders. I just need one piece of sea glass and then I'll turn around. I won't leave her alone for long.

Sherlock starts howling. I almost lose my balance on a rock and hear a few crunches under my boot. 'I'm so sorry, things that live inside shells.'

I can hear Sherlock, but when I look back I can't see them anymore. That part of the beach has been engulfed in white too.

And finally, a frosted-ice aqua gem peeks up from the sand. I pick it up as if I just won the game of life.

Smiling with relief, I start back. My stupid boots slide on the rocks and I shriek and have to put my hands out to balance. I can hardly see my own outstretched fingers, which is fascinating but also scary as hell.

The light has dropped out of the air, and the previous faintly fishy smell has been replaced by something else, something eerie and indescribable. I try to place it – washing on a wet day, the moment before snow falls, the numbing taste of an ice cube. Everything is shivering, billowing clouds. The waves sound so close I have to check my feet to make sure I'm not paddling. I try to find the second rock to climb but I can't. It isn't where it was before. Sherlock howls again but he's further away and in a different direction.

Closing my eyes, I attempt to get my bearings from the sound of the sea, but it echoes all around me and instead of lapping, it's roaring. My body shakes, my hair is dripping, my clothes suck at my skin. Saltwater seeps into my eyes and makes my vision bleary. I rub at them but that just makes them smart. I'd never thought about it before. The weight of water. But now it's getting heavier with every step.

I think of all the sailors drowned out there in the *Dead Eye* wreck. I think of the bomber pilots. I remember the stories of how quickly the tide takes its victims. I think of them perished with seaweed tendrils of hair and oceans in their eye sockets.

As I am thinking about the dead creeping their way towards me, I feel I'm not alone. 'Snow, is that you?'

No answer.

'Snow. Clap your hands so I know where you are.'

Nothing. There's someone there, I know there is, watching, close. The salt of the sea mingles with the fresh sweat all over me. I'm on fire despite the cold.

'Who's there?' My voice sounds deadened by the space. The fog blinds me, switches directions, comes closer. The hairs on the back of my neck prickle. I spin around but the motion just swirls the fog into new confusing patterns.

Squeezing my hands into fists and gritting my

teeth, I force myself to think rationally. I bet some of the gang have arrived here early. Gwenni maybe, trying to scare me because we aren't friends anymore. She's probably sniggering at me, just out of reach.

'Oh, you are so funny, aren't you?' My voice sounds frail, unconvinced. There is no answer.

I'll get out of this any second and find Snow and Sherlock waiting safely for me.

Without warning, I walk straight into the sea. It soaks up as far as my shins. The water sucks, trying to drag me out. I topple forward, drenching my clothes. I manage to right myself, only to be knocked again by an even bigger wave that slams me into the rocks. I feel sharp pain in my side, my shin, my wrist. I've got to get out of here. I need to keep calm.

Flailing, I grip a jagged edge of rock and drag myself out of the waves. My clothes are so heavy, so cold. I will myself to keep walking, keep the sea at my back, keep up hope. I need to get away from whatever it is that's hiding in the fog. I don't understand how I know it's something bad, malignant, nasty, but I do. I can feel it in the offbeat rapping of my heart.

A sound chills me to the bone, so near it is almost on top of me. Laughter, so close to my ear I can feel its breath. I stagger, my sodden clothes dragging me down. The ground gives way beneath me and I fall, cracking my head, a burning slash of pain.

I see a figure looming towards me.

I begin to believe in ghosts.

Chapter Six

Dragging myself up from the murky depths of sleep, I squint at the diamond brightness. I rocket forwards, ready to fight the unknown. Mam is there to catch me.

'It's alright. Your scare on the beach gave you a nightmare is all.' She cradles me back down onto the pillow. 'It's all OK now.'

My mouth feels clogged, my gums bruised. Mam is smiling, but I can tell it's an effort.

'It's OK, Lark. You're safe.'

Rain drums against the roof of the caravan. Sherlock pads his way up my duvet to lick my nose and I can tell he's been out for a walk because he still has that wet-dog smell.

I shiver, and Mam puts the back of her hand to my forehead.

'How are you feeling?' Dad's face has been full of worry for the past three months. I mentally kick myself for adding to his troubles. I can't actually kick myself because Sherlock has lain down across my ankles.

'I'm fine.' The words rattle through my brain like shrapnel. Mam smiles. We are both smiling and neither of us means it.

'We were worried there for a minute.' Her hand on my forehead is so cool and comforting. 'You've been shouting some very strange things.'

'Have I?' I break out in a sweat. The ghost. They'll think I've lost my mind.

'About planes coming and the sky being full of fire.' Dad is wiping the dishes and putting them away.

'Oh.' My mouth is gritty. 'Weird.'

'I've told you not to watch the news. It's too distressing.' Mam wraps her cardie around her and shoves a screwed-up tissue in her pocket. 'Here, take some of this.'

She helps me to sit up and passes me a herbal brew that has pink spirals of steam rising from it. Our caravan only has two bedrooms, so I'm sleeping in the main living space, on a bench that turns into a bed, so it's pretty awkward for everyone with me just lying here. I would complain about it, but Dad will threaten to make me sleep in a tent outside. I'm alright with tents in the summer but not in this weather.

I sip the shimmering liquid; it tastes of summer evenings and meadows filled with poppies and pinks. 'Snow?'

'She's fine, no thanks to you.' Dad stacks the dishes so angrily one chips, and Mam bites the corner of her lip. She has violet sacks under her eyes and her mascara has run.

'She's outside. Making a den. I told her not to wander far. I know I can trust her. She's not been any trouble.' Mam puts the emphasis on *she's*. I think of the den in the woods and shudder. The Witch Woods. Ridiculous. I push away dark images.

I close my eyes and think about the fisherman who helped me off the beach and brought me back here. Away from the cold and the mist and the ghost. The ghost. I tell myself my eyes were playing tricks on me in the fog. A shiver bubbles the length of my spine.

'You were lucky you fell above the tideline.' Dad always scratches his stubble when he's cross. 'Who knows what could have happened to you if you'd been in the water.'

I heard a girl's laugh out there in the fog. I'm sure of it.

'Totally irresponsible.' I can tell by the way he's avoiding eye contact that Dad really wants to have a proper go at me, but he doesn't want to upset Mam.

He's right, of course. Mam gives me a sympathetic look and a wink which sticks her eyelashes together for a second. It makes me want to bawl.

'Why don't you go and get some air?'

Dad raises his eyebrows as far as his hairline. 'In this?'

It's raining a lot. Proper, full-on, fat Welsh rain.

Mam hands him his oilskin as an answer. He shrugs it on, gruffly acknowledging when he's not wanted. 'I guess I'm going for a walk then. Walk, Sherlock?'

Sherlock looks at him and then nestles down again. He double hates the rain.

'Looks like I'm on my own.'

When he slams the door, Mam sits next to me, close. 'Did I ever tell you our story?'

I nestle back. We both know that she has, a zillion times over. The words are beads in the necklace of a well-threaded tale. Each glimmers and sparkles and glows. It's a story she used to tell me when I was a kid and I've heard it a thousand times. I love it anyway. It makes me feel better to hear how Mam-gu is the oldest grandmother ever to pick anyone up at the school gates. And how when Mam first picked me up the other kids called her my nan. They both had lots to do with their lives before they decided to have children. They made the most of the world so they could fill us with knowledge when we came along.

She tells me how Mam-gu travelled from the aurora of the polar lights to the ancient secret tunnels beneath Byzantium. How Mam was called Saffron River, because she was born as a monsoon hit a bazaar in India and the paths ran with yellow-gold spices. Then come the stories of how we were named: she says I was born at dawn in a nest at the tip of the forest's tallest tree. Larks rose all around us to sing me a welcome. Snow was born in a field at the stroke of midnight while stars began to fall as flakes of snow from a sparkling winter sky.

It's a good story, I'm not saying it isn't, but we were born in a hospital in Cardiff like practically everyone else we know and so was Mam. I've seen the birth certificates. Mam-gu likes to see herself as a free spirit but she used to work in the tax office and hasn't travelled far. I've seen all of her photos and they are practically all in Wales. Also larks nest on the ground. If the story was true, I would have been called Rook or something. But Mam does love to craft a spellbinding tale from absolute thin air. I have a feeling it's a version of a story Mam-gu made up for her.

Her voice is thick with tiredness, but her face is bright. I like it when she gets lost in storytelling.

I can't concentrate for long. Everything makes me think of the beach. The rain on the metal walls and roof has me back there, drowning. Every shadow outside is the face of the spirit who laughed. The clock pings and I almost jump out of my skin. I don't want Mam to pick up on my fear, in case she thinks it has something to do with her, but I can feel it radiating from me.

Right at the bit where Mam starts telling me how the rain hit the floor so hard in India that you weren't sure whether the water was travelling downwards or upwards, there is an unidentifiable noise outside. She puts her finger to her lips. We hear it again. Somewhere between a wail and a squeal, like an animal caught in a trap.

'What is it?' The words judder out of me.

We listen on tenterhooks to the wind and the trees, then jolt when the noise comes again. Mam dashes to the window and flicks open the blinds. She is through the door so quickly I don't have time to stop her. Sherlock is straight out after her, barking his most ferocious bark. I hear yelling, throw off my duvet and hurl myself into the pouring rain with my teeth bared, ready to face whatever it is.

It's Mam who's yelling. Snow stands there, with a woman holding her by the arm. Snow is making that inhuman, animal wail and for an insane second I am happy that she can still make a noise when she wants to.

She looks scared. Mam is screeching and jabbing her finger at a woman I don't know. The woman is not letting go of Snow's arm. Snow reaches out to Mam. Mam tries to catch her hand and her favourite silver bangle flies off her wrist and circles through the air, spinning and glinting like the moon.

'Let go of her.' I rush straight at the stranger,

bringing my arm down hard on hers, so she has to let Snow loose. 'What are you doing?' I push Snow to Mam, who catches her and pulls her inside. 'Who do you think you are? Assaulting a little girl like that. Get out of here or I'll kill you. I'll kill you. Do you hear me?'

I'm shouting and shouting, and the words start to blur, as they do when I'm caught in the sharp fangs of rage. The woman steps back and slips into the wet mud. She picks up Mam's bangle and holds it out to me.

'Get your hands off my mam's jewellery.'

She drops it and holds her hands up in front of her face as if she's afraid I will hit her.

'Lark, calm down.' Mam is shouting at me now. Snow is peering out from the door of our caravan. Sherlock is yipping and trying to get out of her grasp. I'm soaked and coming back into myself.

'Ten.' Mam starts me.

Ten, remember to breathe.

Nine, the woman's eyes are so scared.

Eight, the sky is purply grey.

Seven, I should help the woman up. I hope I didn't hit her.

I break Mam's hold and go towards the woman, but she scrambles up and backs away.

'I came here to warn you.'

Six. Warn us about what?

'You don't belong here.' She looks around her, terrified. 'You don't know about this place.'

Five. Don't know what about this place? I wish I could ask but the anger is still too strong, and I have to concentrate on the counting to get back to normal.

'You don't know what you're doing.'

Four.

'Bad things will happen.'

Three.

'You don't understand. I'm trying to save you.'

Two.

'Please leave. Please.'

One.

'She will come for you.'

Zero.

'Who will come for us?'

I get no answer. The woman gives me one last petrified look, then turns and runs. I snatch Mam's bangle up from a puddle and Mam grabs my hand and drags me back into the caravan.

'Lark, get out of those clothes and dry your hair. I need to look after your sister.'

My fingers are trembling badly. The woman's words repeat themselves over and over in my head. *She will come for you. She will come for you.* I try to stop myself, but I can't, and I just manage to make it to the bin before I throw up.

'Lark. Are you OK in there?' Mam opens the door. 'Oh, Lark.'

She holds my hair. When I've stopped being sick she puts her hand on my head to feel my temperature again. 'You really shouldn't get so angry, sweetheart.'

Which is rich coming from a woman who was just screaming like a demon of the underworld.

'That woman is probably just not very well.' Mam hands me some tissue. 'We'll keep an eye out, but I don't want you to stress about her.'

I wipe my mouth. 'She's completely nuts, obviously. But what did she mean, *she will come for you*?'

'She was just talking gibberish. You are not to worry about it. I'll try to find out who she is and you just keep your wits about you and stay away from her if you see her. We'll report it to the police if we spot her again. OK?' Mam takes the bin of sick into our tiny shower room and clunks about as she empties it down the toilet. 'We'll make sure that Snow isn't left alone for a while. And, Lark?'

'Yes?'

'Don't tell your father. He's got enough on his mind as it is. Now, can you check on Snow while I get changed please, lovely girl?'

'Course.' I feel light as a feather when I get up and the floor comes up to meet my feet. It's an odd feeling. Like I'm going to float.

'And put the kettle on for some hot chocolate.'

I have to do everything.

Snow is wrapped in my duvet with her face lit up by the light box. 'You alright?'

She nods.

'That woman was a bit freaky, right?'

She nods exaggeratedly and rolls her eyes.

'You're not to be afraid of her, OK? I'll protect you.'

She gives me a look that tells me she doubts it and receives a friendly punch to the arm in return. I flick the kettle on while she goes back to her artwork.

'That's beautiful.' The light box has calmed her down really quickly and she looks far less traumatised than I feel. I check through the slats of the blinds again, just in case, but there's nothing there but the hammering rain, the trees bowing to the wind, the purple darkness. The kettle clicks itself off and I jump, then try to laugh at my own nervousness. Making us all hot chocolate helps to settle me: the routine of it, the comforting smell, the memories it brings back that drift through the air.

I take ours over to the table and sit next to Snow, who starts slurping immediately. I congratulate myself on having topped it off with some cold milk, otherwise she'd be picking bits of shredded skin from the roof of her mouth. 'Do you mind if I have a go?'

She pushes the light box along the table to me and I try to think of something calming to make with the pieces of sea glass. There are more bits here than I found. Snow must have collected some on her own while I was lost in the fog.

I start to rearrange the pieces into the shape of a boat. The sound of Mam having a shower and the rain still drumming on the roof helps to soothe me. I was right, this is therapeutic.

'What do you think, Snow? Pretty outstanding seascape, right?'

She wrinkles up her brow to show she doesn't think that much of it.

'Cheek. What have you drawn that's so good, then?' I'm only joking. We both know that whatever she has drawn will be brilliant. I take a gander.

She's drawn us on the beach. You can see the cliffs on one side and the town in the distance on the other. There's me, her holding that horrible doll she found, and Sherlock with his nose pointed up to the sky like he's howling. She's done small blue dots to represent pieces of sea glass, and a big puffy cloud thing for the fog. She moves her arm so I can see more of the page and my heart skips a beat. Almost hidden by the fog is a figure. A girl in a green dress.

'Who is that, Snow?'

She is engrossed in drawing a large candy-pink jellyfish.

'I said, who is that?'

She swaps colour for the jellyfish's tendrils, which annoys the hell out of me.

'Was there someone else on the beach?'

She smiles and continues her blue squiggling worm shapes.

I move the sea glass about into a different arrangement while I try to rationalise. The light box makes Snow's face glow and spills over her drawing. Mam is getting out of the shower. It's my last chance to ask about that girl in the fog but, I'll be honest, I'm too scared.

I look over at Snow's picture again and breathe out loudly with relief. She's covered the figure with scribbles of grey and has drawn in a mermaid in the sea. She is just using her imagination. I was using my imagination too when I heard that laughter. We've always been brilliant at making things up because it doesn't cost anything.

'Hot chocolate and then bed, I think.' Mam's face glows from the warmth of the shower.

We sit listening to the rain as we cradle our drinks and I lose the twitchy fear which has been picking at me all day.

'Teeth.'

She doesn't have to tell me. I've been brushing my teeth for years now without a reminder. But I just nod and let her be a mam for once.

I try not to look at my reflection when I get to the mirror, but I can't hide from the something that darts about at the back of my eyes. It's that creeping fat spider of doubt. Doubt about my sanity, what I saw, what was real.

I try to concentrate on more normal things, like how my nose is the wrong shape and my eyelashes too stubby. I spit crimson whorls of blood into the sink and I know I need to be good to myself for a bit. I stare into my eyes and make them look savage, brave and determined. It very nearly works.

'Night, Lark.' Mam barely has to raise her voice to shout this through the door.

'Night, Mam.'

As I come out of the shower room, Snow is closing the curtain to her bedroom. She peers at me through the crack before she shuts it. It must be my state of mind, but it feels like a seriously creepy thing to do. Mam has left a lamp on for me and so Dad can see when he gets in. My nightie is laid out on my bed and next to it there is something that I really don't want to see.

The doll stares up at the ceiling with its empty, expressionless eyes.

Chapter Seven

Sherlock wakes me up, scratching at the door to get out. I'm amazed I managed to sleep at all. All night, everything that has happened kept trickling through my thoughts like icy water.

Because I am in the main living area Sherlock wakes me up first, which is a total downside. On the upside, he sleeps next to me, curled up against my stomach or in the crook of my legs. Dad must have come back while I was sleeping. It scares me that I didn't wake up. I checked the door was locked about fifty times before I lay down and would have put something across it as a barricade if he hadn't been out. Though I'm not sure any barrier would stop a ghost. I glance up at Snow's sleeping area. Her curtains are still drawn.

Very quietly, I open the cupboard where I stowed the doll last night and am relieved to find it's still there. I know dolls don't really come to life and kill people but if any doll was going to this would be the one.

I shut the door on it again.

Open it to check it hasn't moved. Shut it again.

Open it and hide the doll even more thoroughly. Shut it again.

Shrugging on my coat, I let Sherlock out into a startlingly bright morning. The rain has stopped and every puddle is a mirror of the bluebird-blue sky. I step down from the caravan and close the door behind me softly, not to wake anyone.

Sherlock sniffs the ground like the detective he is and picks up a scent that takes him down to the stream. I follow him, feeling the lemony sun waking up with me, watching the way the stream glitters and eddies, running yellow and clear in parts, black and secretive in others.

'Sherlock. This way. There's a good boy.'

Listening to the chorus of every bird trilling, I chase the water down to the sea. Today, in the light, I can be sensible about my fears.

Fact – I was tricked by my senses in the fog into thinking there were unearthly things there. The figure coming towards me must have been the person who rescued me. The way he looked must have been distorted by the freaky conditions.

Fact – We found an old ruined house in the woods. There must be old, ruined houses all over the place. If someone else told me they were scared by an abandoned house, I would totally taunt them for ages.

Fact – Snow found a doll that is way creepy but is still just a doll and is now hidden inside a suitcase until I have a chance to get rid of it completely.

Fact – That woman had serious health issues. That's why she was being so mean to Snow. She probably needs to see a doctor. We'll probably never see her again. And if we do I'll be ready.

Facts always make me feel better. Fact.

My certainty quivers as I get to the beach. Mam and Dad are still asleep. Face your fears head on. I remind myself that Snow drew a mermaid, so that's how realistic her pictures are. Taking a huge gulp of sea air on our side of the Forbidden Beach, I feel stronger again with each fresh breath.

'You see, Sherlock. There's the place where I fell over. There, on The Others' side.' There are a few people with dogs on both sides of the beach today, but even though I just have my coat over my nightie and my knees are bare above my wellies, I feel like the sun will have made them friendly, so I carry on walking about.

'This is our side, Sherlock, but if you want to go across No Man's Land you can.' He is already bounding off to make friends with a caramel-coloured labradoodle. They look comical, circling each other and trying to sniff each other's bits to say hello. My grin is broad as I watch them bound across the freshly tumbled sands, letting the clean, rinsed world warm me with all its beauty and peace.

'We *are* going to be alright. The sea air will work its magic…'

A commotion behind me makes me turn, like everyone else, to see the rest of our friends arrive in a trail of cars. They are beeping their horns to tell us they are here, which is completely embarrassing. My tummy tumbles as I think of Gwenni and how spiteful we've been to each other, but it also means that Mam-gu has arrived and if anyone can sort me out she can.

I pick out her car immediately.

'Sherlock. Come on. Good boy.' It doesn't take

much coaxing to get him back. He loves being with people. His tail spins in circles as he races back to the caravan park. I run too. It'll be good to be surrounded by noise and jostle and hum, and I also want to put some proper clothes on, so I don't look a complete dork.

I try to sneak into our caravan, so I won't be seen in my nightie, but the sight of Mam-gu makes me forget.

'Mam-gu!' I run to her and launch myself into her arms, breathing in the hotchpotch floral craziness of one of her homemade perfumes, loving her loosely tied bun and the scent of cinnamon and knowledge that always wafts around her.

'It's good to see you too.' She laughs her throaty laugh and hugs me hard. 'By the sea at last, eh, Lark? And what do you think of it so far?'

'I love it.' And at that moment I do.

'And your mother?'

'She loves it too, Mam-gu. We all do.'

'What's wrong?'

'I need to get dressed.'

She laughs like it's the best joke anyone ever told, then realises I'm serious and lets me go.

Dad comes out of our caravan looking rumpled and with a big sleep crease up his face. We laugh at him and he laughs at himself. The others arriving is a tonic. I wave to a few people as I go in to change. They all wave back cheerily except Lorelei. She nods sarcastically and smirks. She makes me feel three years old, which is her favourite thing to do to people, but I have more important things to worry about than her.

Charlie, Gwenni's brother, waves and I wave back and mouth, 'I've been reading loads.' He lent me loads of books back home. He is a serious bookworm. The first thing he'll do here is find the bookshop and spend a small fortune. He does it everywhere he goes.

He gives me an enthusiastic thumbs-up which makes me really happy.

Snow is watching TV and Mam is singing and drying her hair with a hairdryer.

'They're here, Mam.'

She turns her hairdryer off and I have to repeat myself.

'Do you think I didn't notice?' She's laughing. Snow laughs at something on TV. I laugh as I try to get my wellies off where they've stuck to my feet. We're all slightly hysterical at the excitement of everyone else arriving. I want to spend time with Mam-gu before I see anyone else.

I dress quickly and keep my head down as I go into Mam-gu's caravan. She's not there, so I take a minute to look at all the things I adore so much. Her bobbled green cardigan, the scarf with the pictures of cats, the keyring with the ducklings painted on it I made for her when I was six. She's brought her photo album, of course, it goes everywhere with her. I keep trying to tell her she should scan them all into a computer but she says she prefers them this way. Beyond her blinds, people are hugging and shaking hands and slapping each other on the back.

'Lark.' Mam-gu comes in carrying Marple, her fat ginger cat. Marple studies me, her eyes slits of lime. Seriously, why couldn't she have gone to a cattery for the week? I go to stroke her then think better of it. Sherlock is her arch-enemy and just a whiff of him brings her claws out.

'There's something bothering you.'

'Not really.' I'm kind of worried I might be being stalked by a phantom.

She gives me her infamous withering glance. Then she goes searching for her glasses.

I sit politely, every now and again offering half-hearted suggestions like:

'Perhaps they are in your bag, Mam-gu?'

'Did you use them for reading?'

'Have you left them folded in your book?'

She goes into the toilet, to see if she left them in there. I shout in to her, 'Can you remember when you last used them?'

She crashes out, holding a Sylvia Plath. 'Used what now?'

'Your specs, Mam-gu.'

'Ah yes.'

She's forgotten what she was looking for. She's getting more forgetful. I guess her mind is too full of things to fit them all in any more.

Wiley Riley starts banging away on his bongo drums outside and a few of the others strangle a pop song with him. The erratic bangs make my head thud. Why did he bring them?

'Found them.'

She lights a joss stick and sits opposite me at the small table. She's brought a special chair for her back so she towers regally over me and I feel like an infant perched on a bench. I wish I hadn't come.

'So, what's wrong?' Her glasses accentuate her stare. I love Mam-gu to bits, but I'm a goldfish bowl when she looks at me that way and I know she can see all my thoughts swimming about in my head like guppies. I consider telling her the truth. That I'm terrified. That I'm not sure what happened to me out in the fog. Will Snow ever speak again? Who was it on the beach and will they come back? What am I supposed to do about life, the universe and everything?

'Oh, you know...' I squeak.

'I know.' She thinks I want to talk about my mam. Of course, she does. But I already know. You can't hide the smell of illness, however hard you try. It permeates everything: the air, the taste of your food, the smell of your clothes, the sugared-almond mornings and the screech-owl shattered nights.

'I'll warm the pot. The tea will tell.' She pours steaming water from the kettle into a chipped yellow teapot and moves it in circles, humming as she does. I wish she'd get a move on. Of course, I don't believe in her tea-leaf reading claptrap but I play along because it gets her to say what she thinks and I am close to the edge today so anything is worth a go. Most days now I can feel my temper bubbling just beneath my skin. Pretty soon I'll have to count down from a hundred to get back to calm.

'Here you go. Drink it while it's hot.'

The tea is bitter and scalding. I hardly ever drink tea because it tastes so disgusting.

Mam-gu bursts out laughing in chesty boom, boom, booms at my face. 'Not used to tea without teabags are you, my angel?'

I don't bother to argue. Mam-gu won't accept that anyone doesn't like tea. I just smile past the tea leaves jammed between my teeth.

'Don't worry. Swallowing half the tea leaves won't change the reading. What will be will be.'

She clucks and takes my cup from me, patting my trembling hand. From her face, I can tell that she is going to feed me some nonsense about how my mam is happy with her lot, or how fate will take care of the future soon enough. I'm wasting my time here. I've made myself feel foul and vulnerable for nothing. Her jet-black hair has a silver stripe at the parting. I don't know why she doesn't just let it be grey, it would suit her. I study her while I get the chance, the shadow created by her high cheekbones, the dent in the very centre of her forehead, the way her skin is so white you can see every vein running through it in different shades of blue.

I wipe sweat from my brow. Everything tastes of salt. I think if I coughed, salt would spurt up from my lungs and sprinkle the table with white. Marple lies down on my foot, which she absolutely never does. She's so heavy my foot goes dead. That cat hates me.

Just as I wonder if Mam-gu has fallen asleep with her eyes open, she bends, peering even more closely at the remnants of the leaves.

I'm starting to feel like I'm going to upchuck. The smell of mixed perfumes and cat is too strong, and the joss stick smoke stings my eyes. I'm about to make my excuses, when her head snaps up like a kingfisher with a catch. She stares at me and the cup clatters as she places it down.

'You have to go back there, Lark. You have to help that girl.'

Chapter Eight

Mam-gu's words have shaken me to the bone but I pretend I'm OK and slip outside. Dad is banging away at the engine of Wiley Riley's gold VW beetle, which died as soon as it got here.

'It's working again.' He raises a spanner triumphantly and I pull my best leave-me-alone-or-else face. Now I'm thirteen I can put a lot of my moods down to hormones. I watch him test-drive it to the edge of the field where it conks out.

When I get inside, Sherlock comes for a pat, then returns to Mam's room, where she has gone back to bed. She is sleeping all the time at the moment. Even when she first gets up she complains that she's exhausted. I check on her through the crack in the door. Snow is curled up next to her, transfixed by that rancid doll which she cradles close. The suitcase I hid it in has been left open on the kitchenette counter.

Snow's light box is still on and there are pieces of sea glass scattered all over the floor. She must have been collecting them again to have so many, which is annoying as hell seeing as it was my idea in the first place. I pick them up and put them into an empty Quality Street tin we've emptied between us in the last two days. If she can't look after them then I'll have them for myself.

On a scale of one to ten – one being calm and ten being the Incredible Hulk – I'm at about an eight. I can't wake Mam up, so I'm going to have to go out somewhere before I start throwing things about. I smuggle the tin out of the caravan and hide it behind one of the wheel arches, where Snow'll never find it. It's a spiteful thing to do, but spiteful is how I'm feeling.

There is a lot of stuff going on outside. We've taken over six caravans between us all. Mabli Jones, Jake the Idiot's sister, is the newest baby. She is being pushed about in her pushchair by Betsey-Anne and Leila-J, who is seven and acts like she is my age. This will be to give Jake the Idiot's mam a rest. She is going to be watching TV and putting her feet up for the week and nobody better disturb her or else.

I give Mabli a little tweak on her cheek as I go past, and she gurgles and then goes back to sucking at a felt ball, which is only held together with baby spit by the looks of it. My anger goes down to seven looking into her sweet, podgy face and I start to feel guilty about hiding the sea glass. Leila-J starts singing to Mabli a song about a blind man who got murdered. Chills run through me as her thin, sweet voice fills in the air.

Despite the morbid song, I'm glad to see so much hubbub and bustle. It distracts me from that cold, haunting presence on the beach. Accidentally, I come face to face with another cold, haunting presence.

'Alright, Lark?' Gwenni has the face of a bulldog chewing a wasp, a sour lemon and a stingy nettle at the same time.

'Superlative, thanks. Though I don't know what it's got to do with you?' I walk straight past her. She follows, which is completely riling.

'What's it like here, then?'

I know a white flag of peace when one is waved, but I'm not ready to forgive her for dumping me for Jake the Idiot. 'You can see for yourself, can't you?'

She knows me better than anyone else, outside of my family, and can tell I'm at a seven, because she backs up a couple of steps and gives me some space.

'I just thought you might have insider info is all.'

'Apparently not.'

'OK.' She bites the skin around her thumbnail and if I wasn't so angry I'd feel like a right cow. 'Charlie is looking forward to seeing you too.'

This twangs a nerve. Charlie, Gwenni's way cool older brother, has been giving me lessons so I can improve my education. I want to be an avian vet when I'm older and that doesn't come without lots of hard work. He's the only one who treats me like an adult. I'm gutted I've not been able to meet up with him properly since me and Gwenni fell out, but it's awkward seeing him without running into her. 'What's that supposed to mean?'

'Nothing. Just that he hasn't seen you for a while is all.'

'Yeah. Well.'

Jake the Idiot throws a hammer up in the air and manages to catch it. He crows like a cockerel. Gwenni rolls her eyes.

'Looks like your boyfriend is waiting for you, Gwenllian.' She hates being called by her full name. I'm pushing up to an eight again. 'What's he doing? Wow. I think he is actually trying to nail his foot to the floor. Good catch you've made there. Well done. Seriously. Well done.'

'I'd like to see you do better.'

Jake hears her and crows again. I don't even answer. I turn and walk the other way. Gwenni tells Jake to shut up.

Ten, you are not allowed to go ballistic.

Nine, where can I go for a walk on my own without getting into trouble?

Eight, no way am I going to the beach after what Mam-gu said about helping that girl.

Seven, remember to breathe.

Six – AAARRGGGGHHH!

There's a tug at my sleeve and I practically karate chop Snow in the jugular. 'Do you have to creep up on me like that? Stop being so totally weird!'

Her face crumples and I feel bad immediately.

'Oh, Snow. I'm sorry. I don't know what's wrong with me. Hormones, I suppose.'

She takes my hand and I think again how much more grown-up she is than I am.

'What have you got there?'

She opens her satchel to show me some pictures she's drawn and a dreamcatcher. I can guess where she wants to put them. 'Come on then. Let's go.'

We leave the caravan site behind. I feel a sense of power in being the only people who know about the ruin. The woods are stunning today in the after-rain light. It's a good thing to put distance between me and other people when I'm feeling like this. A jay screeches above, the watchman of the woods.

'Here we are.' The ruin would be hard to find if Snow wasn't walking straight to it. She's cut back more of the brambles when she's been playing here by herself and she holds back what's left of the tangles so I can slip through.

Inside she has tidied, which seems like a ridiculous thing to do in a ruin, but with the sun wavering through the canopy overhead and the leaves flittering down from the trees, it looks quite magical. Snow starts putting her drawings about the place. She's covered them in clingfilm, I guess so they won't get damp.

There's nothing scary here today. I don't know

what got into me last time. It's just a fairly standard old building. I let Snow carry on prettying it up and go out to kick about the perimeter, checking out our surroundings. It's so tranquil.

I think I can hear the sea, so I close my eyes to listen better. Yes, there it is, faint but definitely there. I can hear a pipe being played too, the sweet strains of an old Welsh song I've heard the adults sing many times when they have parties. Wiley Riley plays the tin whistle really well. However much I've scoffed when the others are around, here on my own I can really appreciate it.

It's a song about Wales in the olden days. About the hills and the mountains, the rivers and lakes. It's about people working with the land, being proud of who they are. It makes sense to me here in the woods instead of in someone's kitchen back home. My heart swells to the size of a boulder. 'I understand,' I say. To all of the people who inspired the lyrics. 'I understand.'

I open my eyes. There's someone watching me. I see her, flitting through the trees ahead. Two large round glittering eyes. Inhuman eyes. Staring. Gone.

My brain tilts like a ship at sea, then rights itself. It was a mask. She was wearing a mask. I scan the trees, sweat pouring down my back. I didn't imagine it. I know that I saw someone. A gas mask. That's it. One of those war things.

A branch cracks and I spin round too fast. I can't see her, but I can feel her creeping slowly towards me.

'What do you want?' The air has stopped moving. Even the trees are listening. 'I know you are out there.'

I concentrate on not passing out. I feel like a butterfly caught on a barbed wire fence. I turn to see if she's behind me, in front of me, to the sides, then take deep breaths to try to get hold of myself. I sense someone right behind me and turn to stare straight into a mask. I scream.

And then I realise the mask is laughing and has pink-tinged hair.

'O.M.G.' Lorelei likes to say things in capitals. 'That is SO funny. Your expression!'

She pulls the mask up onto the top of her head and I watch any street cred I ever had disappearing faster than the marks it leaves on her skin. She is in hysterics, but not the kind that make you want to laugh with her. The kind that make you want to slap her.

Jake the Idiot comes out from behind a tree and barks with laughter. Lorelei pretends she is having difficulty pulling herself together, so she can prolong the humiliation for me. She bends over with her hands on her knees as if she can't support herself.

'What are you doing here?' My words are bullets. I wish they were real ones.

Her breath comes in fits and starts as she gloats. 'Talking to yourself, were you?'

She stops laughing long enough to do an impression of me. 'I understand. I understand.' Then falls about in fits again.

This is all too much. I am too weary to move.

'Fancy yourself as some kind of fairytale princess out here lost in the woods?' Lorelei is still eking out the laughter, though it fizzled out a while back. JTI is barking, but with effort. I feel simultaneously like kicking off massively and going to sleep.

I start to move past them. 'I can't be bothered. See you around.'

'Not if I can help it.' She throws the mask at me and I catch it as a reflex.

I've seen gas masks before, but I've never actually held one. One of the eyes is cracked and it feels more rubbery than I'd expected. It's creepy in the way all old war things are. 'Where did you get this from?'

'It was on the floor over there, Princess.'

'I'm no princess.'

'That's right cos if anyone is it's Lorelei, innit?'

JTI is such an idiot.

'That's totally right, babe. Like totally right.' As well as using capitals, she also thinks she lives in Beverly Hills. She does my head in, but it's hard to hate someone you've known your entire life and she has had it tougher than most, so I let these fake things slide. That's just the way she hides herself away from all her problems.

She becomes absorbed in tapping her phone, as she does pretty much non-stop every single day, even when she can't make it link to the outside world.

'Who was that girl talking to Snow?'

My knees give slightly. 'What girl?'

Lorelei ignores me, so I look to JTI. He shrugs and starts to clean his nails with a penknife.

'I said what girl?'

'We saw them just now. Playing over there.'

'What do you mean "talking to Snow" anyway? Snow doesn't talk, remember?'

'Are you calling me a liar?' Lorelei puts her phone down, a sure sign she is annoyed.

'I'm just stating the facts.'

'Well. Whatever. Enjoy yourself out here in the woods. Try not to get freaked out, won't you.'

'Woooooooo!' JTI rushes at me with his arms up in the air. I pretend I'm not bothered. They go off into shrieks of laughter again.

'Come on, Jake. Let's get out of here and go somewhere interesting.'

They disappear off to find their next victim and I rush up to the ruin, praying, praying, praying that nothing has happened to Snow. Perhaps she is talking again. But who was she talking to? My heart skitters around as I listen hard at the doorway. Hearing nothing, I go inside. Snow's pictures flutter on the breeze and her dreamcatcher lies on the ground, forgotten. The doll is propped up in the fireplace. I pull a face at it and pretend I'm not scared it will react. There's no sign of Snow anywhere.

'Snow?' There's nowhere to hide, it's way too

small. I walk around to the back. The woods are denser here but there's a vague path or animal track, so on instinct I take it. Sure enough, a short way down there is a clearing. Snow is standing there, motionless.

'Snow. Are you OK? Lorelei said she saw you playing with someone?'

She is standing over something. A bird. A brown lady blackbird. It's dead. From the way it's lying, I can see that its neck is broken.

'It's OK, Snow. Sometimes birds die. Perhaps it flew into a tree by accident or just got tired and fell.' I remember picking up an exhausted swallow once and carrying it gently in my hands to safety. 'We'll bury it nicely, alright?'

Snow shakes her head vehemently. Snot drips from her upper lip. I find a tissue in my pocket and clean her up.

'OK. We'll just put some twigs and leaves over it and wish it a safe journey onwards.'

She seems happier with this, so we start gathering. 'Snow, Lorelei said she saw you talking to someone.'

I wait. Snow arranges ochre leaves in the shape of a flower on top of the tomb of twigs and bark.

'She says she heard your voice.'

Snow hesitates and then carries on adding brightly coloured leaves to her funeral decorations.

'And she saw you with a girl.'

Please say something. Please just speak, so that Mam can be happy. We can sort anything out if you will just talk.

Snow doesn't reply, so I don't push it any further. Maybe she is almost ready to talk and if I carry on she will stop forever.

We finish placing all the leaves and twigs and berries like a teepee over the bird and hold hands to make a wish for its safe passage.

'Come on. Mam will be wondering where we are.'

As we make our way back down the wending path, Snow turns to wave.

'Are you saying goodbye to the bird?'

She firmly shakes her head.

Chapter Nine

'Oi, Lark, you div. It's your turn.' *Div* is a polite choice of word for Lorelei.

'Dare.' I can't tell the truth about anything at the moment. It makes the space under my chest hurt. There's the terrible danger it might make me cry and I never cry in front of anyone but Gwenni, so since we've fallen out I never cry. She is avoiding me, which means she is stuck indoors.

I get a huge cheer for choosing a dare. We all know the truth about each other, we have known each other all our lives, so there aren't really any questions worth asking anyway. And they've all got it in for me because they're blaming me for being dragged here instead of going somewhere they might actually want to go. I guess they are all overjoyed at the thought of scaring me as revenge.

We are sitting around a little fire we built on the edge of the beach and everyone's eyes gleam in the flames. There's just us. All the adults have squeezed into Mam-gu's caravan for a 'party'. They only check on us occasionally because they are caught up in their boring conversations.

It's Halloween, and we are on holiday, so the old people cut us some slack with curfews. We've trick-or-treated around each other's caravans and bobbed apples. Lorelei held JTI's head under the water for a bit too long, which is a seriously childish thing to do. Outside the party, pumpkin lanterns are smouldering and the air is a bittersweet stink of wax and singed fruit. We've been warned off starting the proper bonfire, though we might be allowed one for Bonfire Night, so we are crouched around this small fire and grumbling about how pathetic it is.

Lorelei is dressed as a witch, which is apt. Tonight she is in one of her vicious moods. It's something to do with the way she gets treated at home.

'What shall we make her do, girls?'

I don't know why Lorelei is always in charge. Probably because she has the biggest gob.

'Snog one of the boys!' Jake the Idiot is the only one who votes for this. He is the only boy here.

85

He's dressed as a zombie, his costume made entirely of toilet roll. His zombie head disintegrated with the dunking Lorelei gave him, but he still has scrags of it left in his hair. He gets laughed at truly and properly, and probably for a bit longer than is necessary.

'Don't be dull.' She is all demonic eyes and wickedness. 'I dare you to go into the woods.'

There's no response to this. Everyone is watching me. You could chop through the air with a woodcutter's axe.

'Sounds easy so far.' I need shooting. Really, I do. Thank goodness Snow has been put to bed because she isn't feeling well, otherwise she'd run straight back to fetch Mam and I'd be in it up to my neck. If Gwenni was here she would stop this.

'Go into the woods. Only...' She pretends like she is mulling something over. 'I've heard strange stories about what goes on out there in the middle of the night. So, actually, perhaps, on second thoughts, it's better if you don't.'

I have a full audience now, so I have to keep acting like I don't care. 'You've only been here about five minutes. How have you heard stories already?'

It actually would only take Lorelei five minutes to find out all the local gossip. She's like that.

'Oh, you know. Just here and there. Rumours on the wind. Little birdies everywhere.'

This is a reference to earlier taunts about my name. I don't rise to it, because that's what she used to say: look out, Lark is rising to the bait, her temper is flying, don't ruffle her feathers – that sort of endless junk.

She does her best to look mysterious. She's pretty good at it, being a complete and total drama queen.

Everyone draws closer. I try not to, but I do all the same. There's something about her. It takes a good bit of persuading to get her to carry on and she loves every last second. The fire crackles and shoots sparks up into the dark night. The world presses in on our circle of light and binds us together.

'Once. Not so very long ago. The ghost of a girl stalked the children of this place.'

I scoff loudly. This is what I do when I'm afraid.

'Well, if you are not going to listen...'

Everyone gives me reproachful looks and Leila-J hexes me. Charming.

'Go on with your *story*.' I really emphasise the word to make it sound pathetic. 'I'm sure it will be *fascinating*.'

Lorelei carries on as if she can't even hear me. I was hoping I would start a fight and she'd forget about the dare, but she sees right through me. This is going to be extra terrifying, just for my benefit.

'She wasn't a wizened old hag.'

'What does *wizened* mean?' Betsey-Anne is all saucer eyes and hugging herself.

'It means having a face like a raisin, which she clearly wouldn't have if she was a *girl*, would she? That's pretty obvious.' I am still trying to ruin Lorelei's moment.

'It doesn't matter, because she wasn't. It was the ghost of a child. A child with the face of the dead. Hollow, soulless eyes. A spiteful mouth. Gnarled fingers that hooked into live children and cut them into ribbons of blood.'

Jake the Idiot grabs the nape of Betsey-Anne's neck and she jumps so hard she falls off the rock she's sitting on and almost into the fire. We all roll about laughing. I don't know why someone nearly setting themselves on fire is so funny, but it is.

Maybe because it takes our attention away from our own fear.

'Look. I'm trying to tell you what happened for your own protection. So, shut it. All of you.' Lorelei's face is alive in the flickering flames. Threads of her hair dance on the breeze like Medusa's. Smoke catches at the back of my throat and my eyes stream. I can't believe I'm afraid of this theatrical tosh but I am. I really am.

'She seeks children out with a corpse candle.'

'What's a corpse candle?' Leila-J huddles close to Betsey-Anne.

'It's a candle that signals death. If you see it, it means you are going to die.'

I bite my thumbnail off so low my thumb stings.

'She wanders about looking for a friend to take back to her lair in the woods.'

This touches a nerve and I can't help glancing over at the woods. I know where Lorelei is talking about. She's using it against me and it's working. I've been in a pretty ropey state since we got here, and All Hallows' Eve isn't helping. I think of Snow tucked up in bed and flex my fingers to stop them jittering. My leg shakes so visibly I have to hug my knees up to my chest. I yawn to try to cover this.

'If they tried to run away, she hunted them down and locked them in the cellars, where the walls dripped with blood, and their screams for help could be heard deep into the night.'

A branch snaps in the fire, making us all jump, and there is another ring of the kind of laughter that comes with the creeps. We quickly fall silent again. Lorelei stays quiet too and gives fearful looks towards the woods which are horribly convincing. She loves to drag out the pain.

'What happened to the kids?' asks Leila-J.

'She left them locked in there. Clawing at the walls till their fingers bled to the bone. Screaming to get out. And eventually...' She fixes me with a gloating eye. 'Eventually, their screams just died away.'

We all pretend to not be bothered. Jake the Idiot takes out his pocket knife and inspects it. I scoff again, then lick my lips and yawn unnaturally loudly. Betsey-Anne huddles even further into herself and says, 'Whatever,' under her breath.

'But that's not the worst bit.' Lorelei relishes

attention, even if she has to scare the bejesus out of us to get it. 'Some nights, when there is witchcraft in the air, the girl decides she isn't satisfied and comes back to take more children. She won't be satisfied until she has taken every single one and killed them all.'

'Bull.' We are all hooked, dangling like fish. There's something strange about the atmosphere tonight and her words spin around us in the festering black. The wind picks up and the pumpkins grin brightly. A fox howls far off in the distance.

Lorelei is staring directly at me. She knows she's won. 'If you don't believe me, Lark, look in the mirror and say "The Ghost Girl" three times.'

'What happens?' The words hurtle out of my mouth and hang there in the smoky dark. I wish I could reel them back and stuff them in my pocket.

'I'll tell you if you make it back from your dare.'

I laugh again. It's completely for show. Everyone else groans.

'I don't think that Lark should go.' Leila-J is either very brave or very stupid to stand up to Lorelei. JTI dribbles, in shock, I think.

'It's fine. I'll go.' I have no idea why I say this. I have no idea why I say this. I have no idea why I say this.

'You have to go through the woods to find the ruin of her house and take a photo of it on your phone as evidence.'

At the mention of phones, nearly everyone gets theirs out and checks for signal. There still isn't any.

'Yep. No worries.' I've been much braver than this lately.

'Good luck then.' Lorelei takes her pocket mirror out and trout pouts at herself. 'The Ghost Girl. The Ghost Girl. The Ghost Girl.'

That sow. I let my jacket fall off one shoulder as I walk towards the woods and keep looking at my phone screen, like this is the easiest thing in the world. The others probably can't see me as soon as I step outside the circle of light, but I do it anyway, in case.

As soon as I get into the woods, the dark is so intense I can hardly see my hand in front of my face. I use the light of my phone to see where I'm going, but it means I can only focus on the bit just in front of me. The others were whispering when

I left, but they are laughing now. Thanks, so-called friends. Thanks a bunch.

Ducking behind the first line of trees, I decide to hide. I'm not going any further. Not because I'm scared, exactly. More because I don't like being told what to do. I'll take a photo of the ruin tomorrow and adjust the brightness, so it looks like night.

Scrolling through the photos on my phone helps to distract me. Pictures made with sea glass and a light box. Selfies of Gwenni (my ex-best friend) and me. She would have come with me into the woods, if she'd let me go at all, but she's been hiding in her caravan all day. There's one of Mam-gu that time she chained herself to a sessile oak to stop them cutting it down. One of Mam feeding ducks. Laughing, the way she used to.

I turn the phone off and find myself in abject darkness. I turn it back on again and try not to panic as it boots up.

Peering through the trees, I can see that the others are starting to drift off to bed. I'm glad. Although they are all betraying me, it also means I can sneak back soon.

There's a decaying dank smell in the woods at

night. The puuusssh-shusssh of the sea on the wind's breath. I'm more alert to noises than I ever am in daylight. That terrible fox scream in the distance again. Was it a fox? What if it was something else? Something worse.

I know these thoughts are pathetic and childish, but I can't stop them. Strange shapes skulk in the shadows, moving silently towards me. I concentrate on my phone screen. Of course, looking into my phone means that my face is lit up, so anyone or any *thing* that wants to kill me will be able to find me easily. Gah! Shut up, stupid brain.

Checking on the fire again, I can see it's just Lorelei and JTI left. As I watch, she reaches into her bag and comes back up wearing that sodding gas mask. She knows I'm watching. I turn my phone off and move, to see if the glittering mask eyes follow me. They do, so I hide behind a different tree and stay there. When they go to bed, I'll sneak back to my caravan. I just wish they'd hurry up.

It's getting seriously cold. The leftover light is thin and the shadows stretch and shift into witch-hunters, monsters, ghouls. There are things in that dark I can't explain, hidden in the darkest dark, like they hide in the fog. I press my back against a tree, so no one can sneak up on me from behind.

Lorelei is still at the fire. For a second, I hope that something will happen to me, just so she can feel guilty. The feeling passes pretty swiftly.

I think back to my run in with Dad earlier. I had a go at him because he wasn't listening to me. I feel disgusting. I concentrate on being scared of the woods, of the noises, of the stories that weave themselves through the dark nooks and crannies, of anything that will fill the sadness inside me with something else.

Peeping around the tree, I see Lorelei leave the fire. She's left the gas mask behind, sitting where she was, as if it deserves its own space. The others have all disappeared too.

Hah! I win. I'll just leave it two seconds to make sure she's gone into her caravan and I'll be free to go back.

Damn. Someone is coming from the other side of the site. Now I'll have to stay here till they've gone. It's hard to tell who it is from here. I wish they'd get a move on. They are walking so slowly.

No, walking isn't the right word. It's more unusual than that. As if they are gliding or drifting, which they can't be, obviously. My eyes are playing tricks on me again. It's so dark, but it's someone small. Probably one of the other kids, ordered by Lorelei to come and get me, to flush me out of the woods. The figure walks up to our caravan, right to Snow's window, like it's peering in. I should cry out, but something holds me back. I don't want whoever it is to see me. Snow's light goes off and I can't make out the figure anymore.

Now I can move, and I run. What if the intruder has gone into our caravan? What if it is Snow sleepwalking? What if the darkness has seeped into our lives?

I stop outside our door. It's ajar. We always make sure it's tightly closed at night to prevent Sherlock from yowling at the moon.

When I go in, Sherlock is upside down, sleeping with his paws in the air and belly undulating. Surely if something bad was happening his hackles would be up? I pull the door to behind me. Everything else is quiet.

Creeping across to Snow's bedroom, I see a crack of light under the curtain. She sometimes has a night-light, but instead of that blue-white plug-in bulb, this is a yellow glow, quivering. I don't want to go in there. There's a spanner left on the table from when Dad was fixing the Beetle and I grab it. I have to look. I have to face my fears.

I draw the curtain back. Snow is sleeping soundly. She has a candle burning right next to her, which explains the yellowy light. It's so dangerous in such a small space she may as well be tinder. Mam and Dad would flip out if they knew she had it in here. I check around again. Behind me, to the side, on the ceiling even. Picking the candle up, I turn and let out an almighty yelp. There's a girl there, coming towards me with a corpse candle in her hands, she's…

It's you, you stupid idiot, your reflection. The relief makes me melt and almost pee myself.

Licking my fingers to snuff the candle, I check that Snow is still sleeping. She is. Mam is too, though Dad must still be over at Mam-gu's. The doll is awake with its horrid blank eyes. It stares at me from the safety of Snow's arm.

'And you can shut up as well,' I say to it. My voice makes Snow flinch and turn over, and I see the edge of something poking out from under her pillow. I pull at it, kidding myself I'm trying to make sure she's comfortable.

It's a bundle of papers clipped together. I flip them over and have to sit down on the floor before I fall. They are all pictures of her with a girl I don't know. She's wearing a green dress. In every drawing she's gripping Snow by the hand as if she is taking her away. The girl in the green dress is the one Snow drew in the fog. The same size as the figure outside our caravan. The same size as Snow. And she's staring from every page straight at me with hollow, resentful eyes.

Chapter Ten

'Come on, Sherlock!'

I haven't slept well, unsurprisingly, and I'm not in the best mood when Dad sends me out with Sherlock to keep an eye on Snow, so Mam can have a rest, as if she doesn't rest all the time. Dad still doesn't know about the strange woman and Mam seems to be on a far-off planet most of the time so she hasn't stopped us going out without supervision. I feel like I'm bringing myself up sometimes.

My shoulder feels as if it is on fire where Sherlock's lead keeps nearly pulling my arm out of its socket. He keeps trying to tug me back or stops completely and refuses to move. He usually only does this when there is a hailstorm, or he's tired, but today he is trying to convince me to go back to the caravan. I can't help the creeping feeling that he has some kind of sixth sense and wants to stop me going near the ruin. I know that's where Snow will be. She is obsessed by the place. Sherlock sits down again, and I tug his lead too hard and make him breathe in that struggling way that makes me feel rancid about myself. I *cwtch* him sorry and he licks my nose in forgiveness. He is still reluctant to move.

He turns on his best doleful puppy-dog look and I consider taking him off his lead and letting him shoot back without me, but I can't. I'm too scared.

'Come on, Sherlock. You need the exercise, you lazy thing.' And I need the company. I give him a bone-shaped treat and he's slightly easier to drag along for a bit.

It's a bit warmer today. My top is flimsy, and I can feel the sun through it as we shuffle our crackling way, kicking up leaves like confetti and snapping twigs underfoot, and under-paw. Sherlock loves to snuffle his way through the fallen leaves and chase the floating ones. Against my better judgement, I decide to set him free, so he can enjoy scuffling about.

'You stay with me though, Sherlock, OK?' He strains at his collar as I try to get him to look me in the eye. 'I'm going to let you off now, but you have to stay close.'

He darts off into the piles of leaves, scattering them everywhere and a laugh bursts out of me. It's so bright and the sky is so, so blue and everything is crisp and clean. The unnatural thoughts of last night seem ridiculous in this glorious sunshine wood.

'Come on, Sherlock. Here, boy.' I set off with renewed vigour. I'm an intelligent, strong human being. So my sister is a bit extraordinary. Isn't everyone? Most people are downright oddsville.

Sherlock patters beside me happily now, his tongue lolling sloppily. I make up a song in my head about how fantastically powerful I am and how I'm not afraid of anything.

I am cool. I am strong.

There is nothing in me that could ever do wrong.

I'm alright even though I usually play by the rules.

I'm not all that unusual. Not all that unusual.

It's not the best song ever invented, and it's more than a bit repetitive, but it's joyful all the same. If I was a singer I'd sing my song out loud to celebrate how brilliant stuff is. I'm not a singer, by any stretch of the imagination.

The guilt comes crashing back and I feel ashamed for being happy, what with Mam and everything. It's like that uncontrollable cold feeling when you come out from swimming. With the guilt comes the fear again.

Sherlock stops on high alert with his tail pointed straight as an arrow and a growl rumbling deep in his throat. I think he's picked up on my change in mood.

'Come on, Sherlock.' I make my voice extra loud to compensate for being chicken-hearted. Sherlock prowls very slowly behind me. It'll do. I don't care if he's grumpy as long as he's with me.

There is nothing to be scared of, I keep telling myself, trying desperately to remember the words of the song I made up only a couple of minutes ago.

You didn't imagine anything, a voice in my head says. *That thing on the beach, in your caravan, in the ruin, is a ghost and she's come for you. She's come for all of you. She's come for Snow.*

I tell my brain to go away. I decide to push all of my Snow worries out of my head and appreciate my surroundings instead, like old people always tell me to.

There's plenty to admire about the woods here. There are the most beautiful trees: sycamores spinning out helicopter seeds and silver birches with opal skins shining, and the air is so full of birdsong that it's a wonder it doesn't drop out of the sky onto your head like a hat.

My scuffed brown boots pinch a bit. Thanks, Gwenni. She will soon realise how much she misses our friendship and we'll be mates again, if I'll let her be. It isn't her fault she thinks that she's fallen in love, so has completely dumped me as her friend.

I hope that massive zit on her chin splats puss all over Jake the Idiot's face.

When we get to the ruin Snow isn't there, which is so far past irritating I can't even begin to see irritating in the distance.

'Snow.' Nothing. I raise my voice and try again. 'Snow!' There's no sign of her. 'SNOW!'

I startle a pheasant up out of the undergrowth in a clatter of scarlet and green. I laugh with relief as it rattles away from me. Sherlock bolts off in shock. So much for him being a trusty companion.

Sudden silence. There is no birdsong anymore. It's as if someone has turned the volume down. I stamp the ground to check I haven't gone deaf. Everything feels twisted, upside down, odd. I try to whistle for Sherlock, but my tongue is sour and dry.

'Sherlock!' *Something's scared him off.*

The silence presses in on me. The air glimmers and shifts. A branch cracks and falls straight out of the sky, making me swear. I look up to see why it fell, there's nothing but a cathedral of trees. I straighten my spine, grit my teeth and 'collect myself', as Mam taught me to do.

Perhaps there are no birds singing because they don't want to stick to this dingy part of the wood on such a gorgeous day. They've all flown to the brighter bits and are warbling merrily there. I should follow their example. Trying to sweeten my voice, I call Sherlock again and offer him a treat, even though I've run out so it's a lie. I'll pay for it next time I try to get him back on his lead.

'Sherlock. Come here. Do you want a snack?' Nothing. No rustling. No barking. He never disappears. He's always somewhere. 'Sherlock, Sherlock. Come here. There's a good boy. Please.'

And then I see Snow. Far off but close enough to hear me. I practically screech at her, 'Snow.'

She disappears through the trees. She's running fast. I run after her. What she's running from? I've lost her. My breath rasps. I wish I was fitter. Where is she? Snow?

There she is. I catch a glimpse of her just up ahead and give chase, calling her name until I haven't got enough breath to shout again. Branches tug at my clothes and rip my hair. I see light ahead. A flash of sun. The snowflakes on Snow's coat. I crash in that direction.

The cacophony of noise as I burst out of the wood is deafening. I stumble back so fast I fall, rolling and pressing my face to the earth in shock.

If I had carried on running, I would have gone straight over the edge of a cliff.

'Are you alright?'

I squint up into the face of the woman who threatened Snow.

I snap, 'What are you doing here? Get away from me.'

'I'm not doing anything. Honestly. I'm just checking you are alright.'

'What have you done to my sister?' I'm ready to fight this time.

'Nothing. Really.' She backs away, hands in the air.

I stagger up and edge back from the clifftop. 'Leave me alone.'

'You seem distressed. I can get you help.'

She's talking to me, but she's looking past me back into the woods as if she's expecting to see something there.

'Just leave me alone, OK? Just leave us alone.'

She takes a step away but doesn't leave. There is a blanket spread out nearby, with a book open on it and a pair of binoculars. 'I like to sit here and watch the world go by.'

'How very interesting,' I say with buckets of sarcasm, even though I can understand why she would want to be here at the edge of the world. She is the woman who attacked my sister and I'm on red alert.

She says, 'I told you to be careful.'

I go into battle full force. 'Look, just don't go near my sister again, alright. Or I don't know what I'll have to do to you, but it won't be in my control.'

'She likes sisters. She took mine.'

Rooks chatter in the trees behind us and we both whip our heads round. We turn back slowly, ignoring our simultaneous reaction.

'What do you mean?' I can hear laughter drifting up from the beach.

'The girl. She's trying to take your sister, isn't she?'

I feel dizzy again. 'I have no idea what you're on about.'

'She took mine. All those years ago. She was only sixteen. We never saw her again.'

'Never saw who?' The world is slow motion, marshmallow, spongy.

'My sister. The girl in the green dress took her. She's lonely.'

I hear laughter again and lean to see. Snow is down on the beach, giggling and skipping. She looks up at us then laughs and turns to run.

Chapter Eleven

I've sat with Mam for a bit this morning. She is having a good day so hasn't cried at all and has managed to stay out of bed. She even ate some breakfast. I've been showing her our sea glass collection and photographing the prettiest bits with my phone. We've been trying to look at the world through them though you really can't see much. They make everything seem hazy and liquid, like a dream. Mam said they made everything ghostly. I managed a very weak smile.

Snow has gone out with Dad and Sherlock somewhere. I haven't spoken to her since I nearly ran over the edge of the cliff. I can't get it out of my head that Snow wanted me to fall. I see-sawed through the night, trying not to think about it, dream about it, nightmare about it.

After a while Mam declares that I'm getting under her feet and sends me out to do something normal like 'find a boyfriend or go and have a chat with Charlie or something'.

'I don't fancy him. OK?' Mam used to help me with my studies but since she's been so ill she's stopped. I don't want to upset her by admitting I've replaced her with Charlie. My face is sunburn-hot as I leave the caravan. I get this terrible blotchy rash up my neck when my parents wind me up. Why they get such pleasure out of making me look like I'm having an allergic reaction I have no idea. Perhaps I am allergic to them. It wouldn't surprise me.

When I get to the stream, Mam-gu catches up with me. 'Lark.' She is a bit out of puff.

'Hello.'

'Very dark night last night, wasn't it?' She raises an eyebrow and looks at me keenly.

'I didn't notice.'

'Dark night. The spirits were at work.' She nods and her eyes pierce a hole in my skull. She passes me a bag with some books in it. 'Take these back to the library for me, will you? I got them out on the way here and I've finished them already.'

I know she did. Everyone complained about having to stop for her while she sorted out a temporary library ticket, thanks to being a fixture at our library at home. I don't want to take them back. They are so heavy my arm feels ruined as soon as she passes me the bag.

Actually, it's unusual that Mam-gu wants me to go to the library *for* her rather than *with* her. She practically eats books, she devours them so quickly. She even has a book necklace with a real mini notebook on it which she gets people to sign their names in. Not celebrities. Just ordinary people. She says they're more interesting.

'OK.' I can't help the sulky note that wriggles out of my mouth.

Mam-gu takes a swig of her homemade herbal medicine from a silver hip flask and coughs. I feel bad for her. She has been ill on and off for a long time and she looks truly unwell this morning. Packing and unpacking again must have taken it out of her. She gives me directions for how to get to the library and cough, hack, coughs again.

'Do you want me to get anything for you while I'm there?'

She shakes her head and wafts me away with her spittle-stained hanky. I'm thrown by the trace of red on it, thinking for a second it's blood, then realise her herbal potion must be red. She has a passion for scarlet ingredients in food, from her beetroot cherry crumble, her rowan-berry omelette, to her blood orange and pomegranate cake. I try not to eat at Mam-gu's. We all do.

I give her the cheeriest goodbye I can and head into town with my head down. I don't have space in my head to worry about her being ill as well as everything else. The path takes me along the side of the sea. Even the velvet-blue waters, a red-sailed yacht far out and a peregrine don't do anything to improve my mood. It's not too far but the string bag Mam-gu has given me is elephant-heavy and awkward and the books poke their corners through it and keep thwacking my shins. I'm in a pretty bad mood by the time I reach the library.

I plonk the bag of books on the counter. The librarian has her head underneath the desk and I give her such a shock she bangs it on the edge as she comes up.

'Ouch. Thanks for that.'

Just what I need. A narky librarian.

She looks nothing like you'd expect. She's young and her hair is dyed bright colours: ruby and turquoise, cockatiel-quiff yellow and budgerigar green. Her glasses are cerise and have diamanté at their winged corners. She has them perched so far at the end of her nose they can't be any good for seeing things.

She scrutinizes me as if I have robbed the Bank of England. 'These aren't your books.'

'I'm bringing them back for a friend.'

'Oh, you know Olwen?' Her face shines. 'Isn't she marvellous!'

'She's alright.'

'She popped in the other day with someone. Charlie. I don't know if you know him?'

I'm about to answer that of course I know him but she prattles on regardless.

'They were both so interesting and they've read so much. She's very wise. Told me that I should trust my instincts and always listen to my heart. I don't know. There's something about her. Like she's pointing you in the right direction without you even knowing it. There was this one thing she said…'

I zone out here, thinking about what the multi-coloured woman has just said. *Pointing you in the right direction.* As much as Mam-gu pretends to be a batty old nag, I've never seen her do anything without good reason. Did she send me to the library to help me find out what's going on?

I zone back in again. The librarian is waiting for some kind of response.

'Can I use the internet?'

'I'm so sorry. Haven't you heard? The mast is broken so we are out of signal.' She smiles cheerily. 'We've taken advantage and switched all our computers off for maintenance. If you want to pop back next week maybe?'

So annoying.

'OK. Do you have any books on local history?'

'Of course.' She takes her rainbow-self off ahead of me. Her boots are the brightest speedwell blue with tiny silver stars on them. I feel jealous. Perhaps I'll paint my brown ones yellow or something.

In the dingiest corner of the library, she points to a small shelf of books that look long forgotten, they are so precisely placed on the shelves and in such perfect alphabetical order. 'Is there something particular you were looking for?'

'No, no. Nothing particular.'

I pick a book at random and leaf through it. She

pretends to sort a few books about on the shelf, but I can tell she's hanging around to be nosey. She puts her hand in her pocket and clips on a name badge. Her name is Enfys, which means rainbow in Welsh and suits her to a T.

'Forgot to put it on.' She smiles at me, clearly hoping to chat.

I turn away, pretending to be studious.

'Well. If you do need anything just let me know.'

I wait until she has rounded the corner. Through the gaps between the books I can see an old man with a comb-over striking up a conversation with her at the desk.

Scanning the titles, I choose one called *The History of Our Town* and flick through it. There are lots of pictures of miners with braces on their trousers and helmets with lamps. Women hanging out sheets and bloomers on lines. I find a horrible story about how a mine under an estuary collapsed, drowning lots of people, many of whom were women and children who couldn't be named because they weren't supposed to be there in the first place. I get sidetracked by it for a bit.

When I remember my search, I delve through the books quickly, tossing them aside in frustration when they turn up nothing. I am about to give up when I see a pamphlet crammed away at the back of the shelf. By the dust, I'd guess it hasn't been read in many years. The photograph on the cover makes me squeal. I have to shove my fist in my mouth.

It's a picture of the site where we are staying. Definitely. The shape is the same, with the stream at its throat and the woods behind.

I huddle down on the floor. My knees feel wobbly. I'm not scared exactly. In fact, the suspense is delicious. It's like being a character in a story. Libraries are so far removed from real life, it's like anything could happen and I'd still be safe.

The pamphlet has the title *The Blitz*. I've heard of it before but I thought it was just in London. On the first page there is a description of the local area, generic stuff. The next page has a photograph of evacuees with tags around their necks and small cases, followed by a page of some cheery-looking women in headscarves working in a factory because the men were all away fighting. The next has a photo that makes my heart stop.

The house is different because it has windows and curtains, a roof, walls and a door, where now there are holes and brambles and Snow's clingfilm-covered pictures. A girl and a woman stand in front of it and they haven't bothered to look happy, the way people usually feel obliged to do for photographs. The girl has a woollen dress on and even though the picture is black and white, I know that dress is green. Snow is such a good artist she's captured perfectly the expression on this girl's face, the slight snub to the end of her nose, her bobbed hair. I clear my throat as if I'm about to make a speech, but it's to dislodge the pure lump of fear stuck there.

Unfortunately, the noise makes the librarian look to see if I'm alright. She's coming over. I don't want to have to explain what I'm reading. I suppose I could tell her I'm doing a project about the war. Or I could be a complete cowardly custard and go and hide in the toilet…

I flick the door to 'Engaged'.

There's only one picture of the girl and I stare at it until it blurs. I flick through and find pieces about local disappearances, mysterious drownings, paranormal investigations. I think of the fog on the beach and wonder how many souls have been enveloped by it, never to be seen again.

I read:

Wales is a place steeped in mysticism. Peculiar stories, unusual sightings, legends and myths, passed through generations in poetry, story and song. Of course, with the landscape being wild in the local area and the forces of nature sullen, we can assume that many unexplained disappearances are due to the treacherous storms and tides rather than suggestions of inexplicable curses or hauntings.

The door rattles and I gasp so hard I almost choke on my tonsils. 'There's someone in here.'

I stuff the pamphlet down inside my top and, flushing the toilet, saunter out as best I can when I am stealing something for the very first time in my life. I'll bring it back.

In the luminous strip light of the library, the librarian has her back to me and the old man is seated in one of the kiddie's chairs reading a newspaper. I feel like I have a massive arrow over my head pointing me out as a criminal. I push open the exit door with sinful hands and stroll through.

As soon as I have made it outside, I pick up my speed. It's dark already, the clocks have gone back; this should help me to get away unnoticed. I jump as someone clutches hold of my arm.

'I didn't think I'd catch you.'

It's the librarian. I pull my arm away.

'You forgot this.' She holds up Mam-gu's string bag.

'Thanks.' I snatch it way too strongly, almost yanking her fingers off. She rubs her hand but I don't apologise. I yell over my shoulder, 'Thanks again.'

'Give my regards to Olwen,' she shouts. 'And to Charlie too.'

I don't bother to answer, which is probably rude of me, but it would be even more rude if I yelled, 'Desperate much?' I rush all the way out to the sea without stopping for anything or anyone.

I'm scared. More scared than I've ever been. I have to do something, but I haven't a clue where to start.

Chapter Twelve

I can hear singing. Not the kind of singing a choir might be involved in or a ghostly, haunting song. More a drunken yob-type singing. The kind of chanting that puts everyone on edge. I breathe deep into my gut and keep my footsteps light. A little way down the beach there is a crowd around a pitiful fire. I was hoping not to run into anyone at all. This really isn't my night.

Of course, they might be nice people on an out-of-season holiday, like us, but previous experiences tell me to be wary. I creep forwards. They're far enough away that they won't see me if I'm careful. One of them is throwing stuff onto the fire to try to get it going properly and the others whoop and cheer every time. The singing is raucous and a tune I don't know. I break into a trot as I pass them. The tips of their cigarettes move like glimmering red insects.

'Alright?'

I stop.

'What have we got here then?'

Two teenagers block my path. They are carrying torches. One shines a beam directly at me as if it's an interrogation and the other, the boy who spoke, shines his onto his face from underneath his chin so he looks like some kind of devil.

I'm suddenly tired. I'm so tired I'm not scared. I exaggerate a sigh. 'Look, I just want to get past, OK?'

'See. I told you. It's one of them.' The boy seems disgusted. I've met his type a few times in the past. He doesn't like me because of the colour of my skin. He hacks up from his throat and gobs at me. I feel wet slide down my cheek. I don't want to give him the satisfaction of reacting, but I have to get rid of it, so I take a tissue from inside my pocket, slowly, calmly, wipe it away then flick the tissue at him.

I start my countdown. Ten.

He spits again but misses. 'Want to join in the party?'

The one who is shining a light in my face sways

drunkenly then drops the torch and scrambles to pick it up.

Nine.

'Not really. I'm quite particular about who I party with, thanks. Also, I like a proper fire rather than that piddling thing.'

The torch dropper giggles. I recognise her. She's one of those girls from outside the shop who I pretended to curse on the first day and she's drunk, but in a stumbling, tipsy sort of way. The boy is drunk in a much worse way. His features are nasty, and his mouth is a bloodthirsty snarl.

'Think you're funny, is it? Think you're funny, is it?'

Eight. He's moving towards me menacingly but I'm damned if I'll give up my ground.

Seven. A nerve twitches at the side of my eye.

'Look. I don't know who you are. Or where you came from. But I just want to go home.' I sound exhausted but reasonable.

He snickers then spits at me again. He misses but flecks of it catch in the sea wind and land on my neck.

Six. I feel the nerve twitch again. The girl loses her balance and the beam of her torchlight judders across my legs. I cement my boots to the ground. I wipe the spit with my sleeve.

Five.

'You don't know where I come from? You don't know where I come from?' He sounds incredulous and more slaughtered than I'd originally thought. This could go a number of ways. I'm counting, but it's not helping to calm me down like it's supposed to. Adrenalin pumps through my body so hard it makes me jerk.

'Leave her alone, Joshua.' The girl slurs her words, but she sounds kind enough. She reels forwards and I reach out to right her.

The boy smacks my arm.

Four. Three.

'Get your hands off her. Do you hear me?'

He shoves me and my feet almost let me down, but I manage to keep them rooted, here where I belong, here on this land which is mine as much as his.

My voice, when it comes, is cool and even. You'd think I was ordering an ice cream. Only I know that the anger raging inside me is stabbing to come out.

Two. 'Listen, Joshua. And make sure you listen

good.' That's it. I'm getting way sarcastic. 'I'm not sure whether you think I have a problem with my hearing or whether you only know about five words which you have to repeat over and over to communicate with your stupid friends, but if you don't get out of my way really, really soon I'm going to have to lose my temper.'

He obviously wasn't expecting this. He actually gasps. 'Is that right? Is it? Is that right?'

'Again with the repetition.'

'Hey, you lot,' he shouts. 'I've found someone who wants to join the fun.'

Things go into slow motion here. He grabs me and hurls me in the direction of the fire. The girl grabs hold of his shoulders and tries to pull him back. The fire has caught the wind and lights up the silhouettes of the gang. I fall forward onto my hands and knees, scraping my palm. The girl is screaming and slapping at him. He throws her off and she falls with a crunch. I hear the sound of her bones as they snap.

One.

There is a large stone under my hand. I jump up, holding it high, ready, and he tips off balance, falling heavily. I drop the stone and help the girl up. She stumbles towards her friends, holding her arm. She's crying and I feel bad for her. He is fine but I only have moments before he will get back up. The singing has stopped.

I grab Mam-gu's bag and go. The torches that fell along the path light the way back. I walk fast but I don't run. I won't give them that.

Something touches my shoulder

'Argh!' I spin round, fists up in front of me, ready to fight again.

'Ssh. Calm down. You'll get us in trouble.' It's Gwenni. I've never been so pleased to see someone in my entire life. I only just stop myself hugging her.

'What are you doing out here?' I snap.

'I could ask you the same thing.' She is equally stubborn.

I want to tell her everything. About the fight just now. About the ghost. 'Just walking.'

She lets me not tell her. Sometimes she's good that way.

'I'll walk with you.' She doesn't link her arm with mine like we used to. Things have changed. I say something sarcastic to try to make things normal. 'Lovely evening, isn't it?'

'Yeah. The actual best.'

I sigh. It's been a long night. I need all the friends I can get.

'This is dumb. I'm annoyed cos you dumped me for Jake the Idiot because he is, well, he's an idiot and I was your best friend and you dumped me … and, well, I'm mad about it. Really, really mad.'

There I've said it. Not very eloquently, but I've said it. Gwenni will probably never speak to me again.

'You're right. He is an idiot.' Although she's partially hidden by the night, I can tell that she's choked up. 'He's been going out with Lorelei behind my back.'

This doesn't come as a surprise. I've seen them together enough times. But Lorelei, of all people. Twice last year she scratched different boys' names into her arm with a compass. That's the kind of girl she is. How could he give up Gwenni for someone like that? I laugh, 'OMG and JTI. The perfect couple. They can talk to each other in capital letters the entire time.'

'I know.'

I don't know what to say. I feel glad that he has dumped her and I'm not proud of it. I don't say anything for a bit. Sometimes if you don't have anything nice to say…

The gang from the beach are out of sight. We would hear them from here if they were coming after us. I like to think that boy's prejudices were altered forever by my courage, but it's more likely that he is too drunk to follow. I must let these things pass quickly, so they don't eat me up from the inside out like parasitic wasps. I watch the waves crest then tip themselves back into blackness. I can tell from the movement of her shoulders that Gwenni is crying. She thinks the sea will cover her sniffling, but I've known her for so long we could be in a battlefield and I'd still be able to pick her out. I take a deep breath. 'You should have known he was an idiot by the fact he is known as Jake the Idiot.'

She laughs. 'Good point. Well made.'

We walk home with our arms linked tightly.

I go to tell her about the ghost, but as the words reach my tongue I eat them back. I'm not sure why. Perhaps I don't want her to think me crazy or I don't want to break this happy spell. It is the two of us together as it was for years and it makes me feel comfy.

We get back and part ways. I go into our caravan quietly in case Mam's sleeping and so I can wash off the blood from where I've hurt my hand before anyone sees, but there's a note to say they've popped out for a moment with Sherlock. Someone's singing behind Snow's curtain. It's one of those old wartime classics that they always play when there's a Sunday night drama. Snow must have a friend in there. A weird friend, granted, to be wanting to sing those old songs, but then most of Snow's mates are weird.

I poke my head in through the curtains without announcing myself and find Snow completely absorbed in her drawing.

'Who was singing?'

She shrugs her shoulders.

'Just now.' I search around her space, which is the size of a thimble, as if I'm going to find anyone there. 'I heard someone.'

I know our walls are thin, but it didn't come from outside.

Snow does the finger, thumb, circle thing to say OK, which translates as, OK, you oddball.

'What are you drawing?' I snatch her picture up. It's yet another one of the girl in the green dress. 'Why are you always drawing this girl?' I'm fuming. I grab her other drawings, scrunch them up, then cast them to the floor. 'Why can't you just be normal?'

I leave her picking up the drawings and smoothing out the creases and go to rest my head against the table in the living area.

Mam and Dad choose this time to reappear.

'Kids.' Mam pokes her head through the door. 'Lark. Snow. We've got a surprise for you.'

Snow comes out and we manage to avoid acknowledging each other without Mam noticing.

'Ready?' She opens the door properly to let through a scampering bundle of fluff, with the most pointed ears you could imagine and no sense of direction or knowledge of how not to bump into furniture.

'A puppy!' I squeal it for both of us and Snow drops to her knees to catch the gorgeous little gremlin of a thing, while I fuss Sherlock, who looks more than a little miffed. Then we swap, and I love the wriggling, scratchy, furry ball of joy immediately.

'We know things have been difficult lately and she needed a good home.' Mam is so happy. 'A man in the pub had five he needed to find homes for and those eyes. We just had to get her.'

'Your mam insisted, and you know what she's like when she's decided on something.'

Dad gives us each a piece of paper to write our suggestions for names on and we mull it over for a good while because a name has to last a lifetime. Finally, we put our screwed-up pieces of paper into a bowl and Mam picks one with her eyes closed because she is the only one we all trust not to cheat.

I won last time. This time Snow gets the choice.

Chapter Thirteen

The next day, it feels like autumn has given its place up for winter. Not the sparkly snowing glamour of winter but a dense grey day which snaps with cold. The caravan site doesn't weather this too well. Mamgu puts her clothes out to dry and takes them in damp and salt-stained. Mabli Jones has a horrible cough, the poor dab, so Jake's mam stays in her caravan. If you ask me, she never wanted to come on this holiday in the first place. I don't blame her. Dad has a mood on and Mam seems blank.

'Get out from underfoot, Lark.' Dad is like a caged bear when he is worried, which is often. 'I can find something for you to do if you need a job?' I think he is suffering worse than Mam with the pain of seeing her ill.

'I'll go out, Dad.' He stands with his back to me and doesn't say anything. I pat him on the arm awkwardly. 'Don't worry.'

I lace my stupid broken boots while Narnia tries to chew them. I know Mam would get me a new pair if she noticed the state they're in, but she hasn't noticed anything for about a year and I don't like to ask. Sherlock hides his head under a cushion. I won't be having company today then. Narnia is too young to go far yet. No bother. I could do with being alone.

There's very little sign of anyone out and about. Snow is off playing somewhere.

'Alright, Lark?' Gwenni is leaning against the boot of their car, sulking. They get dragged around car boot sales and markets wherever they go. 'We're late. Supposed to be the crack of dawn. Charlie forgot to set the alarm.'

'I tried my best to get us out of it.' Charlie winks at me. He looks at us both teasingly. 'Friends again, then?'

He is only four years older than us, but he acts like it's about ten. We let him get away with it because he is super, super smart.

'Ignore him.' Gwenni's having bubblegum for breakfast by the looks of it. 'I'll see you later.'

They are bundled into the car behind Gwenni's parents. Gwenni waves and blows a candy-pink bubble so big it hits the window and splats all over her face. It's a brief exchange but it is some kind of ordinary at least. I wave back and watch the car until it disappears.

'Hello, Lark. You alright?' Mam-gu looks tired as anything today. Her clothes are ruffled, and her skin is papery and lined.

'I'm fine, thanks.' I do my best to look innocent. 'Just going for a walk.'

'Is that right?'

I nod quickly. 'And to get some sea glass. I'm working on a collage.'

'I see.' She sits down on her stoop and Marple slides up to her, ignoring me completely. Mam-gu strokes her head adoringly and whispers to her, 'Lots of old stories in the air today. I can feel history catching up with us, Marple.'

Even though she speaks to the cat, I know her words are directed at me. I don't know why she doesn't just tell me what it is she is trying to tell me. I almost confess all the things that have happened, but I don't know where to begin, so I stroke Marple instead, which is a mistake pointed out by very sharp claws. The cat moves away smugly. Mam-gu seems to be lost in thought, so I leave.

I spot Jake the Idiot with Lorelei. She is filming herself on her mobile, coyly twirling her ratty dip-dyed hair around her fingers. Jake the Idiot looks at her like she is some kind of goddess. Although I'm glad that Gwenni is friends with me again, I can't help feeling annoyed that he has gotten over her so quickly. I give them my best scathing look. Lorelei finishes her video at that moment, which is unfortunate. She glowers at me. 'What are you looking at?'

JTI doesn't have his own mind so he turns and glares to support her. He probably thinks she'll like him better if he acts like her slave. He's probably hoping she'll add Jake to her compass arm.

Lorelei can be malicious if you get into a scrap with her. But I can't come off as a complete coward in public.

'What? I'm not allowed to look at anything anymore, am I?' It's a risk to backchat her.

Luckily, today she doesn't think I'm worth bothering with. She just flicks me the v then goes back to her phone. It would be typical if she was the only person who could get a signal here. Jake the Idiot sits down by her feet and starts trying to light a fire with two sticks as I walk away.

Wiley Riley's car is still conked out at the edge of the field. The mizzle has started to seep into my clothes, so I head to the car for shelter. He hasn't bothered to lock it since it broke down. Knowing him he won't mind if I sit in it for shelter and a bit of quiet.

I yawn uncontrollably. Couldn't sleep a wink last night. I kept hearing someone standing right behind me. As I go to open the door, I can see in the VW's window that I have heavy dark rings under my eyes. I look like a panda and not in a cute way.

I sit in the driver's seat and pretend to drive with the steering wheel, pressing the pedals with my feet. I know it's childish but it's kind of irresistible. Going nowhere quickly gets boring so I watch the specks of rain line the windscreen. My breath starts to steam up the windows, so I can't see out. I feel safe for a change, here in this metal cocoon.

I take the pamphlet out of my pocket. The face of the girl stares out. I pore over the crumpled pages.

The passenger door swings up and I jump and crack my knees.

'Argh! For…' I stop myself before I swear.

Gwenni pokes her head in. 'You alright? What you up to in here?'

She climbs in noisily and waits, chewing on blue bubblegum this time. 'I got out of the boot sale by causing a row with Charlie. Genius, eh? What's that?'

I'm rubbing my sore knees with both hands. I hadn't realised the pamphlet had fallen on my lap.

'Oh, nothing.' I go to stuff it into my pocket, but she grabs it, quick as a flash.

'Wow. How completely dull.' She screws her nose up, then winds her gum around her fingers. 'Why would you want to hide that piece of poo from me?'

Gwenni has always had a way with words. I can't face all of this alone. I'm not sure I can trust her after recent events, but we go back a long, long way. As far back as there is.

'You have to promise not to laugh.'

She laughs immediately. Her tongue is lurid blue.

'I'm sorry. I'm trying to get it all out.' She laughs a bit longer then pops her gum a few times to show she's ready. I can tell she thinks I'm going to tell her about some tedious history project or something.

Once I start telling her, I can't stop. From the first sighting on the beach when I cracked my head, to the nightmares and not being able to sleep. To the ruin, the way Snow is acting, the cliff, the weird woman. All of it. By the time I've finished the sky outside is a storm and rain beats on the top of the car.

Eventually Gwenni breaks the silence. 'Are you on medication?'

It's a joke but we both know it's a poor one and she doesn't know what to say. I wouldn't blame her if she packed me off to a rehab clinic. I'd pack myself off if I thought it would help.

'It's definitely real and I definitely have to do something about it.' I wipe some of the condensation from the windscreen. The world outside looks like a dream.

'Wow. This is way the most exciting thing that's happened in forever. Amazing.' Gwenni has lost the initial stunned shock and is bouncing up and down in her seat like an excited rabbit. 'What are we going to do?'

I could kiss her for her use of the word 'we'.

'So, you believe me?'

'Of course I believe you, you doughnut. Your made-up stories have always been total pants, and this is such a good one. Eek. I'm so excited.' She hugs me and I'm almost glad that I am facing possible insanity because it's glued our friendship back together so completely.

'So, tell me the plan, Stan.' Her cheeks are shining, and her eyes are sparkling bright. I hate to disappoint her.

'I was going to go there tonight and ... and then I was ... I haven't really got a plan as such.'

'Aces. I'm scared.' She doesn't sound scared at all but then she probably doesn't really believe it, deep down. 'What time are we going?'

We decide to meet straight after tea. Routine has fallen apart at ours but it's still going strong at Gwenni's even though they aren't at home. We settle on some items we should take with us, so I spend the afternoon gathering together things from our list.

Dad brought a box full of useful things which are mostly not useful at all. Scrummaging about I find a torch that works if you bang it hard enough and some scratchy rope. I have no idea what the rope is for, I don't suppose you can lasso the undead, but taking it makes me feel better.

We don't have any holy water in our box of useless things, so I get some normal water from the tap and cast a made-up spell on it. I add some of Mam-gu's flower remedies for extra power: larch for self-confidence and pine for self-worth.

I pop back into our caravan to change my clothes for dry ones and to grab a sandwich. Dad welcomes me as if I've been away a hundred years, grabbing me in an enormous hug. I think he feels guilty for being so snappy. He mouths at me to be quiet, which means that Mam is having a good sleep.

Snow is making patterns with the light box and our full tin of sea glass. She found where I'd been hiding it then. I feel so childish. I would have given it back. She turns her blue glowing face up to look at me with a blank expression, then looks down again. I feel every emotion at once and try to let none of them show.

Sherlock bats his tail against the laminate floor of the kitchen side of the caravan and cadges a bit of my cheese. Narnia copies him. The sky outside is stormy violet. Dad switches on a lamp and picks up a book called *Mindfulness and Melancholy*. I don't have time to ask him what it is about. I want to go and look at Mam but I'm worried that I'll wake her. I wonder if I'll ever see any of them again. If I was brave enough, I'd tell them we're in danger. I'd make them leave this place now and go straight back home. Forget we ever came here. But I can't say it out loud. They'll think I'm being selfish, trying to take Mam's holiday from her.

'I'm going over to Gwenni's.' I smooth Sherlock's ears flat to his head, tickle Narnia under the chin and definitely do not look at Snow. Gritting my teeth, I walk out, shutting the door carefully behind me. Half of me feels strong and powerful while the other half feels like the smallest, most insignificant maggot.

But at least a maggot can catch a fish.

Gwenni is waiting for me, leaning against the VW. 'Here goes nothing.' She high-fives me.

She takes the lead. 'OK. Let's establish our POA.'

'What's a POA?'

'Our plan of action. Keep up.'

'Oh.' I let the word peter out on the salty mist, which clings to the trees like petticoats. 'Well...'

'So we still haven't got one?' She chews, something she's always done if she's deep in thought. She stops and grimaces. She's probably bitten her cheek, as she does about fifteen times a month. She practically lives on gum. 'I say we get to the ruin. Find out what the girl is on about and try to convince her to sod off.'

I'm glad I don't have to make all the decisions on my own.

The stream is a nasty cauldron of brown this evening. It must be raining further inland. We go straight to the ruin, me trying not to turn around and scarper.

I know Gwenni isn't taking it seriously at all.

She rasps on about everything the whole way: JTI, Lorelei, what she saw on TV, how she wants to take up surfing, what do I think of the new conditioner she's using on her hair, whether it would be cool to have a Mallen streak put in, how she feels like she's getting better at maths, how she's missing having a phone that actually works. I don't reply because there's really no need when she gets going. Leaves scruffle underfoot and blackbirds squawk out in front of us. There's no way to be silent so we don't even try. When it gets too dark, we use our torches.

'Be quiet, can't you? Isn't your mouth still hurting?' I get antsy when I'm nervous.

'Ooh, alright.' She raises her hands comically then half-complies by talking non-stop much more quietly. You can never get her to give in. It's one of the things that I love about her.

'Wow. I can't believe I've never seen this place before.' She gives her cheek another bashing. 'Oh bums.' She spits blood on the floor and lights it up with her torch. 'Ewww. Hideous.'

A branch cracks under my feet and I leave the floor like I've been electrocuted.

Gwenni giggles. 'Jumpy much?'

When I show her the entrance, she heads straight into the ruin like a kid in a candy shop. I follow, a wobbly-legged foal.

'We'll set up in the middle there.'

I don't know what *set up* means but I nod.

'This is way, way, way spooky.' You can tell she is thoroughly enjoying herself. 'I'm impressed. About as shuddersome as you can get.'

'What do we do now?' I feel like I should be in charge, but I can't think straight.

'First of all, we light candles.'

She gets some out of her bag and we place them

in a circle, lighting them one by one. My hands are shaking so much I manage to burn myself several times.

'This is like that film about the kids who go into the woods and get murdered.'

'What film?' I actually don't want to know.

'Every film. The one with the ghost that is really a batty old woman from the village, the one where the girl is down the well, the one where the zombies arrive in the fog, the one in that big mansion out on the causeway where the woman in...'

'Seriously. Enough.'

Gwenni scatters some lavender flowers on the floor and then sprinkles salt in a circle around us. 'It's to protect us from evil forces. I know it works for witches, so we'll just hope for the best. Come on.'

She beckons me to kneel inside the circle with her. We face each other at its centre and hold hands. I dissolve into laughter. It's nerves not amusement. I don't like to make myself vulnerable.

'Now what's the girl's name?'

'I have no idea.' My tone is petulant. I feel like a

fool. 'She was just known as the German girl. Doesn't seem right, that people didn't even remember her name.'

'Oh. Pants. OK.' Gwenni's already shaky plan has come a little bit unstuck. 'Well, let's try the old "is there anybody there" line then.'

She nods at me, meaning I'm to ask the question. I feel ridiculous talking to nothing, but I do it anyway.

'Is there anybody there?' Even though the words hardly get past my lips, the sound seems to echo off the walls. We wait. The rumbling sea seems close tonight. The wind is shrill. I'm suddenly very cold, then boiling hot again. I think I'm running a temperature. The candle flames leap across Gwenni's face. She's certainly not laughing anymore. It's this place. It has its own memory.

'OK. It's not working. Time for Plan B.'

'What's Plan B?' I'm so relieved Gwenni has thought this through.

'I have no idea.'

'Oh.'

We wait a bit more as if miraculously something will occur. Flickers lick the room, lighting its corners then dancing away, leaving the darkness even darker.

'Why has she appeared to you before?' Gwenni's getting edgy. Whether she believed in ghosts before or not, the mood in this room is closing in on her.

'I don't know, do I? I haven't actually seen her properly.' The sorrow here is encasing us like clay, making it difficult to move.

'There must be something.' Gwenni is panting slightly. She's been known to hyperventilate to the point of needing a paper bag. Candlelight isn't gentle anymore. It's a savage thing that makes everything seem fiendish. She looks so strange, so devilish.

'Or, we could just sit here waiting till death comes for us?'

I'm glad she spoke. I was getting carried away. This room is playing mind tricks with me.

'Are you going to think of something or am I going to have to kill you?' She's joking, of course, but there's a touch of something in her words that isn't jokey. She stares solidly at me. I pick up the water I've cast a spell on and fling it in her face.

'Argh! What the hell…?' It breaks the fear. She

wipes the water away with her sleeve. 'I felt a bit peculiar there.'

'You looked a bit peculiar.'

'Nothing new then.'

Harmony is restored.

'What are we going to do? This place gives me the heebie jeebies.'

'And then some. Give me a minute. Chew your mouth or something.'

'Ha, funny ha.' She does it though.

Bits of sea glass dig into my leg. I've been carrying them around in my pocket. I take the small, scarred pieces and place them in the centre of the circle. They catch the light. If it had been any other time I would have found them beautiful.

A small, almost imperceptible noise chills the air.

'What the hell?' I see genuine terror in Gwenni's face for the first time in our lives.

'Ssh.' Putting my finger to my lips, I listen hard. There's someone here, moving in the shadows just beyond the candle's reach.

Gwenni's mouth is slightly open and I can see her gum in the cave of it, motionless.

There is movement near the entrance. We aren't alone. My eyes dart around the edge of our circle. I want to move further into the light but I have to try to stay strong. Gwenni cowers back and her eyes are feral.

There is a figure. Small, hooded, that's all I can make out. It's staying too far back for us to see it properly.

'Don't cry.' I whisper to Gwenni. Seeing her upset makes me feel stronger.

The wind howls. I raise my voice. 'Why are you here?'

The figure stays in the deepest shadows. I can still make it out.

'What can we do to put your spirit at rest?'

It moves slightly, and I hold my breath. No answer. Gwenni whimpers.

'Come into the light.'

It moves even further into the darkness.

'I'm sorry. I don't know what happened to you exactly but I want to help you.'

There is no response.

'I need you to tell me what you want from me. From my family.'

Nothing.

'I need you to tell me what you want with my sister.'

Ten. Nine. Eight.

'What do you want from her?'

Seven. Six. Five. Four.

'Tell me. What do you want?'

Three. Two. One.

'Leave her alone!' I scream.

An ear-splitting shriek caterwauls through the air and the candles gutter out.

Chapter Fourteen

I will never sleep ever, ever again. Ever.

Dawn breaks, iron grey slices against the pitch-black night. I am still wearing the clothes I had on yesterday and I haven't even bothered to unfold my duvet. The wind is so strong it rocks the caravan. Some holiday this is.

Gwenni was in a kind of post-traumatic shock by the time I got her back to her caravan last night. I'm not sure if she will ever speak to me again. I need to change into new clothes and go check on her.

Mam and Dad are still sleeping. Sherlock and Narnia are in there with them. Snow is in bed with her coat on. She's pulled the snowflakes off it and they are thrown around the place. Perhaps she took my teasing about their being childish to heart. I collect them quietly and put them in my pocket then draw Snow's covers up over her. She's shoved right up against the window, where a draught gets in.

I'm pretty sure she opens her eyes then closes them straight away, as if she doesn't want me to know she's awake.

The caravan site is deserted. The wind this close to the sea is cutting and relentless. I pull my coat around me extra tight and put my head down so the top of my scalp takes the brunt of it. After about two seconds I pull on my much-hated bobble hat. Desperate measures. Most of the time I'd rather freeze to death.

A low whistle. It's Mam-gu whistling for Marple. I go over.

'How be Lark?'

I answer what I think the question is. 'I'm fine.'

I never say fine if I'm actually fine. I don't think many people do.

Marple brushes against my leg, gets a scent of dog and walks away from me disdainfully.

'What are you up to today, then?'

'I'm not sure yet, Mam-gu.' I call Marple, pursing my lips and making that inward squeaking sound cats love. She shows me her bum in reply.

'It's nice to see all of you playing together.'

I can't help the scorn on my face at the word *playing,* but she ignores me.

'Safety in numbers, I always think. You know it's a funny thing…' She pauses.

'What is Mam-gu?'

'Life. Don't you think? How thin the wall between this life and the next is. How things move in circles. Life and death. The leaves falling. The paths we have to tread alone. The memories we leave along the way. We aren't attached to a place. We move through it and beyond. Free souls. Always just passing through.'

I shrug. I have absolutely zero idea what she is banging on about. She starts singing, which I take it signals the end of the conversation.

'Have a nice day, Mam-gu.'

She doesn't bother to reply. It's so unfair how adults can get away with being rude when kids are always told off for it. I pull my bobble hat down. I can see in a caravan window that it looks like a tea cosy, but I need it to keep warm. The wind cuts my face, sharp as a cuttlefish.

I tap on Gwenni's bedroom window because I don't want to wake her whole family. She beckons me to come in.

Tiptoeing across her living area, I notice that she's been threading seashells into bracelets. She likes to do craft things. I let myself into her room, which is about the size of Harry Potter's cupboard. Everything she's brought with her from home is pink all over and frilly at every possible opportunity. Is this why her and Lorelei don't get on so well? Perhaps they are in some kind of pink competition I haven't been told about.

'Wow. You look like poop.' She is her usual complimentary self.

'You don't look so hot either.' Her eyes are bruised, and her face is mottled. 'I brought you these.' I give her the snowflakes from Snow's coat. 'I thought you could make something with them or something.'

'Thanks.'

'Welcome.'

'What are we going to do?' Scared, Gwenni seems like a child, with all her brashness and energy gone. I can't think of an answer, so I put my arm around her. She doesn't comfort me back. I am such a terrible friend, involving her in this mess. I love her so much.

'I told Charlie.'

I hate her. She is the world's worst friend.

'Why the hell would you do that?'

'I don't know. He was here last night when I got in. He could tell I was pretty shaken up and it all just came out. I'm sorry.' Her voice breaks. She looks so tired and forlorn.

'It's alright.' It isn't. 'It's fine. What did he say?'

'At first he thought I was trying to wind him up. Then he asked if we'd been drinking something we shouldn't have been, then in the end I think he believed me. Sort of.' She wraps her quilt around her shoulders. It has pink ballerinas on it. 'Do you think the girl or whatever will come here looking for us?'

I'd really like to say no but all I can manage is an awkward shrug.

'How do we stop her?'

'I'm not sure.' I've been mulling it over since we got back last night quaking in our boots. When the candles blew out, we ran, not looking back but feeling someone close at our heels the whole way.

'Let's just go home.'

'Yeah because everyone will believe us and pack up straight away.' Sarcasm crown for me again.

'What are we going to do, Lark? We have to think of something.'

'I know.'

Gwenni waits as if some stroke of genius is going to come from a place of intelligence deep within me. I wait too. It doesn't.

'I don't know. I really don't.'

There's a soft knock at the door and Charlie comes in without waiting. I take my bobble hat off and flatten my hair with my fingers. Even now Gwenni notices and winks to wind me up. Charlie winks at me too because he winks at everyone. He is holding a battered guitar. He seriously couldn't be any more laid back if he tried. I can feel the heat rise in my cheeks. I can't believe she told him about the ghost. Now he's going to think I'm not smart.

'How are you, lil' sis?' Normally Charlie would get a smack in the chops for speaking to Gwenni like this, but she lets him hug her and tousle her hair, which is sweet but makes me jealous that she has someone to look out for her. 'Feeling a bit better this morning?'

'We are wonderful thanks.' It sounds extra, super pathetic. I turn away and fiddle with Gwenni's books.

'I don't want to be possessed by the devil.' Gwenni sounds whiny, baby-voiced.

'Don't be dull.' I could chuck a book at her head.

'It all sounds pretty horrific. I think you just need to all chillax a bit while we think of a way to sort this.' Charlie strums his guitar. It's irritating and so obvious that he doesn't believe us.

'So what's your plan for today?' He strums again and then twiddles with the tuning knobs. 'It might help to just have a bit of fun for once.'

I do my best to remember fun.

'You can borrow my games console for a very limited amount of time, if you like?'

He has a really old video game thing that he reckons is retro and vintage but we know is just old. Usually he won't let anyone touch it because it is 'irreplaceable'. For some reason, Gwenni lights up at the suggestion. I think she just wants to stay indoors for a bit. He strums again and she looks at me pleadingly. 'Lark? You up for it?'

'Yeah. Of course. Sure.' I can cope with an hour of *The Legend of Zelda* or something. Anything for a break from the worry and fear.

Chapter Fifteen

'Oh My God.' Lorelei's pink hair tips match the colour of her tonsils as she gapes. 'You mean a ghost?'

We are huddled in the VW Beetle again. It is ghostbusting central. Me and Gwenni need back-up and though Lorelei is a nightmare she is also courageous to the marrow. She's in the driver's seat – she insisted that if she was going to spare any time listening to us *sad sacks,* she was going to sit up front. I don't know why she made such a fuss. It's not as if we're going anywhere. Gwenni is also in the front, on lookout for anyone who might sneak up and overhear our conversation. Her glove is sodden from wiping the steamed-up windows.

'Is this just that story I told by the fire?' Lorelei looks up from her phone, her eyes wide. 'This weird woman said there was a ghost girl, that we should stay away, and I just made up the rest. You didn't believe me, did you?' She rolls her eyes.

'No, it's much more than that,' I say. 'And when I saw her that night, when you made me go into the woods, she was looking through the window of your caravan.'

This is not exactly true, but I feel good saying it anyway.

'And I've seen her with my own two eyes,' Gwenni adds, so Lorelei knows that she is far more informed and way ahead in the pecking order.

I can see my breath in front of my face. I'm glad to see it hover there. It means I'm alive.

'Are you for real?' There is scorn but also excitement in Lorelei's voice. We all love the idea of fantasy and drama in our lives until it actually happens. She applies yet more mascara. 'O.M.G. I saw your sister. She was all yucky and snotty and stuff. Maybe she's possessed.'

Snow is in bed with a fever today. I'm not exactly sure what a possession looks like but she certainly looks unusual.

'Oi.' Lorelei hefts open the driver's door and shouts out to someone. 'Get in here.'

I know who it is by Gwenni's reaction. A moment later Jake the Idiot clambers into the back seat next to me. He is wearing a faux-fur deerstalker hat and he looks so completely ridiculous we all burst out laughing despite everything.

'What died on your head?' Gwenni struggles for breath. It's good to see her laughing at something. After a while we stop, but not before we've really made the most of it.

'Listen up, buttercup.' Lorelei commands attention whether you like it or not. 'You're in danger.'

Jake lifts up his earflaps.

We all bust with laughter again.

'Take your hat off, for crying out loud.' Gwenni snorts. Eventually she gets it together but takes way longer than the rest of us. I'm glad she is enjoying her moment of revenge.

'I'll start again. Don't make me start a third time, Jakey boy.' Lorelei's frosted-pink mouth is smiling but it doesn't reach her eyes. She starts to relate the facts to JTI. After a while my mind wanders off. I'm trying to figure out what Mam-gu was talking about with her falling leaves speech. She looked so wistful, so unusual. In my imagination she starts to cry. Her tears run down her face and turn into tiny pieces of sea glass.

'Earth to Lark.' Lorelei breaks my daydream. 'Did you even hear me?'

'What?' My throat feels as if I've swallowed a pond full of brackish water.

'I don't know why I bother with you lot.' She rolls her eyes exaggeratedly. 'I said, and I repeat for the hard of hearing, I want something first. It's time for payback.'

'Payback for what?'

'You didn't do the dare, did you?' She grins at me and I feel my heart palpitate. 'You didn't think I'd actually forgotten?'

I don't bother to answer. Of course, she didn't forget. She doesn't forget anything that serves her needs.

'So, I'll do you a deal. I'll help you save your sister on one condition.'

'What's the condition?'

'The fishermen say you can get a signal offshore and I'm waiting for a text.'

She no doubt fell in love, as she does a hundred times a year, with someone back at school. It must be killing her to be out of contact. I just look out of the window and feel reality blurring with the rain.

'I've found a boat. We just need to go out a little way.'

I take a deep breath and weigh up all the choices I don't have.

'And then we'll come back and … sort out the haunting.'

I exhale slowly, trying to stay grounded. 'What time?'

Lorelei smarms like the cat who got the cream. I can feel Gwenni's irritation, so I avoid looking at her. JTI's open mouth is churning a peanut-butter brittle bar. He splats bits all over my jeans. 'Lorelei really got one over on you there, didn't she? I bet you are absolutely…'

'What time are we meeting?' Gwenni cuts in over the top of him.

'We'll meet at six. Outside the field. If we leave any earlier my mam will go ballistic. She won't notice after tea. She'll be doing her own thing.'

We don't ask what. We all know Lorelei's mam has issues.

'If we all leave at the same time someone is

bound to ask us questions. So we leave separately.'
It's my way of sealing the deal. They all nod.

JTI takes another huge bite and looks about to say something and spray me again, so I cut him off at the pass. 'See you then. Come on, Gwenni.'

She exits the car gratefully and we clasp our clothes to our bodies against the buffeting north wind.

'I'll see you.' We are about to part ways. 'Oh, and Gwenni...'

She turns back.

'Jake really is an idiot.'

I wave goodbye. There's somewhere I have to be. I head into town. I don't have much money, but I have enough for a hot chocolate tinkling about in my coat pocket. There's a little café on the outskirts called The Sun and The Moon and it's easy enough to find from the directions I've been given. The quirkier you are the more welcome you are, by the sound of it. So I'll fit right in.

Tiny brass bells chime as I push the door open, then clank against the flower-painted glass as it shuts. The air is warm and orange and carries the lovely smell of baking. I wish I had enough cash to buy some food. I'll ask for extra marshmallows instead.

I order at the counter. The girl working there looks not much older than me. She's doesn't even glance up from the owl she's drawing on a serviette. I choose a seat in a darkish corner. I want to be able to stay here in the warm for a while without getting kicked out.

A man with long hair sits cross-legged on a wicker bench at the far side. He has taken his shoes off and wears no socks. He's singing a song, until he notices me looking and gives me a beaming smile.

'It's slopped a bit over the sides,' the waitress apologises when she brings my drink. One of her arms is bandaged. It's the girl from my beach fight. Her pierced eyebrows ping up to her hairline when she recognises me. She gets herself together again pretty quickly. 'There's not much you can do about it. The marshmallows make it foamy, I think.'

'Don't worry.'

She goes. Should I leave?

She comes back. 'We've got this new muffin we've been trying. Cherry and cheese. It sounds rank, I know, but it's alright. Have a piece and tell us what you think.'

My scalp prickles. I can't look her in the face. 'I haven't got enough…'

'It's free. We want opinions is all.' She puts a huge cake down on a plate in front of me. 'Enjoy.'

The muffin looks like one of Mam-gu's efforts. Identical, in fact. Mam-gu must have been here, sharing her recipes.

I should've said something to the waitress about the other night. I watch my marshmallows lose their shape and wibble at the edges till they're tiny yellow and pink jellyfish floating in a chocolate sea.

The bells chink. I look up to see who's come in. It's the woman from the library. I try to remember her name and eventually her rainbow clothes remind me that it's Enfys.

She takes her maroon and yellow felt hat off and plonks it down on a table by the window, where its blue and pink feathers catch the breeze. It looks as if the hat is trying to escape. Perhaps it wants to fly to the fashion police.

She almost skips to the counter, places her order for a dandelion tea, then talks to the man about his labrador, who is apparently called Trevor and likes to chew up pillowcases. I pick at my cherry and cheese monstrosity while I eavesdrop.

'They all do that when they are puppies. It'll be a pillowcase munching night tonight. Full moon.' She swings out of her olive-green coat, revealing a swishy purple dress covered with pansies and clouds. I grudgingly admire her courage in clothes. Most grown-ups I know wear brown, black, beige, magnolia and grey.

'Ah yes. The full moon.' He puts on a terrible Scottish accent for some reason. 'A good night for *ghoulies and ghosties and long-leggedy beasties and things that go bump in the night.*' He howls like a werewolf and I drop my teaspoon into my chocolate.

Enfys sits on her own, makes herself comfortable, takes a compact mirror out of her yellow flowery handbag and checks her hair. She looks pretty amazing. I try not to look at my scuffed brown boots. They are everything that is dull and boring and functional in life, right there on the end of my legs.

The bells sound at the door again. I look up and

smile as Charlie walks in. It'll be the first lesson we've managed in ages.

'You're here.' Enfys jumps up and gives Charlie a huge hug.

'Sorry I'm late. I had some kids' stuff to sort out. My little sister thinks she's seen a ghost or something equally idiotic.'

I am going to vomit. Anger burns my insides. He doesn't believe us. He was just humouring us. I tug my coat on.

The waitress comes over and sees that I've only had a nibble of the muffin. 'Oh dear, not so good then?'

'It was foul.' I can't help it. When I'm in a temper I can be cruel.

'Oh.' She looks thoroughly deflated and I'm glad.

I push towards the front of the shop without thanking her and although I can feel my lip curling, I try to keep my dignity by walking past Charlie and Enfys without making a fuss.

'Lark.' Charlie's voice stops me. 'You're here already. You alright?'

I turn and smile sarcastically. 'I'm absolutely fine, thank you. How are you *adults* doing?'

'This is Enfys.'

'We've met before, thanks.' She doesn't recognise me which makes me even more angry. I don't know what's wrong with me. It's like I haven't got any control at all over myself.

Ten.

'Well, I'm sure you *grown-ups* will have a fabulous time here together chatting about *grown-up* things.'

Nine. Seriously Lark. Get a grip on yourself.

'Enfys, this is Lark. She's the one I was telling you about.'

Eight. Breathe. Remember to breathe.

'I think I remember you. I'm just trying to place where we met.' Enfys smiles. I look her up and down and wince purposely.

Seven. 'Don't worry about it.' I turn to leave.

'Don't go, Lark. What's the matter?'

Six. What's the matter? My mam is dying. My sister is possessed. My dad is upset. My mam-gu is talking gibberish. I'm exhausted. Exhausted. Exhausted.

Five.

Charlie turns me to face him. 'Are you OK?'

Four.

Tears burn my throat, my eyes, the back of my nose.

'Come on, sit down. We can chat about anything.'

Three.

I could slam out of the café. I could sit down.

Two and a half.

'Enfys can help you with your studies. I met her in the library the other day and we got chatting. She knows everything. She's amazing.'

She grins. 'I'm hardly amazing.'

Two.

'I'd just like to give you a hand, if I can. Nature is my favourite thing.'

'She certainly knows more than I do.' Charlie beams at her. 'And she can access so much material which will help you. Guess what her specialist subject is?'

'Making her own clothes?' I just can't help myself.

'I absolutely love wildlife.' She is all smiles. 'All of it. Animals, plants, birds. I can't wait to discuss it all with another enthusiast.'

I try to scowl, but it's hard to be annoyed with someone as radiant as her.

One and a half.

'I had a brilliant time in college and you are going to love it. I promise.'

Charlie has clearly told her what we've been doing. All the things he has been teaching me...

He confirms it. 'There's only so much I can help you with, Lark. Enfys is way, way, way, smarter than I am.'

'I don't know about *way* smarter. But smarter certainly.' She laughs. Her eyes sparkle beneath her sapphire-blue glittered eyelids.

One and a quarter.

I can make a choice here. Leave and go my own way alone or stay and trust in someone.

I never trust anyone.

The girl with the bandaged arm comes over and dumps another muffin in front of me. 'It's pumpkin and pineapple. Don't ask me why.'

One.

I sit down.

Chapter Sixteen

Finally, we are allowed to light the proper Bonfire Night bonfire, well away from the caravans themselves and once we've checked there are no hedgehogs or other creatures hiding out in it. We draw lots for who gets to do it and I'm beyond gutted that I don't win.

I'm still spinning from the session I had with Enfys in the café. My mind is reeling with images of birds in the wild and the different books she brought along for me. My first book is about a condor and I'm itching to get going on it.

Mam is doing really well today. She's chatting to Dad and helping Snow with a sparkler. Snow is all wrapped up in multiple scarves because Mam thinks she has flu.

It's only just gone seven and the sky has already been dark for hours but there's a brilliant full moon above us and I'm grateful for it. Lorelei asked if we could try bobbing apples again and then had to apologise to JTI who she practically drowned last time.

'Ready?' Leila-J's mam lights the wick of a rocket, everyone claps and we are all told to move even further back by nervous parents. It's pretty beautiful as it shoots into the sky and splinters into white-blue stars in front of the yellow moon.

There are a few more less successful rockets, some Roman candles, which are pretty dull after rockets, the obligatory Catherine wheel that won't spin, followed almost immediately by one which spins off the fence and chases us all around, which is hilarious and a total highlight. As gasps of delight turn to boredom, the younger kids are taken to bed and we are left to do our own thing.

'I'm going to take a nature walk, Mam.'

She is busy bundling Snow up the steps into the warmth. I've chosen my moment wisely.

'I want to study the behaviour of owls under a full Harvest moon.'

'You'll have to wait for another night then. That's a blood moon.'

I shudder. It doesn't look like a blood moon to

me. It's creamy and pock-marked and appears to be smiling at us.

'Even better. Owl activity is known to increase significantly under a blood moon.' Total lie.

'Fine. But be careful. And, Lark?'

'Yes?' I've already got a few paces away.

'Check on Mam-gu on your way past, will you?'

'Okay.' Gah. Why do I always have to do everything?

Snow gives me the smirk of ultimate smugness before she's pushed inside the caravan. I walk towards Mam-gu's caravan while Mam can see me and then switch direction and hurry away.

Gwenni is waiting for me as arranged underneath the oak tree. She's rubbing her head.

'What's up?'

'Have you ever been attacked by falling acorns?'

'Come on.' We start off towards the sea.

'Whose stupid idea was it to go sailing in the middle of the night?'

'It's hardly the *middle* of the night, is it? What time do you usually go to bed?'

'I think you are missing the point there, Lark.'

'I know. I was being funny.'

'No. You were *trying* to be funny. There's a difference. I brought provisions.' Gwenni has brought crisps and bottled water.

I've never seen the tide so high up the beach. The moon-path really does look like a glistering lane of undulating gold. 'I mean. Come on. That's pretty amazing.'

'It is. And also, amazingly pretty.'

We watch the silken fluidity in silence as we wait for Lorelei and JTI. Bats flit in front of the moon and swoop inches from our heads. The sea breaks on the pebbles and tries to drink the world back with it. Some owls really do use this moon to hunt. I can hear them call and screech.

'Mam says it's a blood moon.'

'Aren't they meant to be red or something?'

'Apparently not.'

'Lark, are you scared?'

'Of what?'

'Everything.'

'Yes.'

There are the twin circles of a couple of flashlights coming towards us along the path. To be on the safe side we duck to the side, even though we are relatively sure who it will be. The flashlights stop close to us and Lorelei attempts to imitate an owl hooting. Gwenni can't resist the urge to jump out at her, making her shriek and swear. I can't really blame Gwenni. Lorelei had it coming.

'Right, we are all here.' Stating the obvious is my forte. I keep my voice hushed even though I'm pretty certain no one else can hear us.

'Well, let's hope that the ghost can't swim,' JTI pipes up. Lorelei clouts him with her phone. I feel a bit sorry for him. In fact, I feel a lot sorry for him.

I switch my torch on and then back off again. With the moon it might as well be daylight. I check around. Still no one about. We have the November evening cold to thank and the ongoing Guy Fawkes stuff.

'Shall we get on with it then?'

'Fine by me.' Lorelei leads the way and Gwenni visibly sulks. 'The boat is moored in the harbour.'

'Are we nicking it?' JTI looks quite excited by the prospect. 'I've hot-wired Wiley Riley's car before. Only when he asked me to, but still...'

'We aren't stealing anything. It belongs to one of my new acquaintances, so we are allowed to take it. Also, it's not that sort of boat.'

'Oh.'

Lorelei clocks him one again. She has a serious problem with violence and he appears to have low self-esteem. I feel bad for calling him Jake the Idiot all the time and make a vow to myself to call him Jake from now on.

I feel bad for not checking up on Mam-gu too. I'm sure she was staying in with Marple because she doesn't like fireworks, but I should have given her a knock all the same. I couldn't because she would have known I was up to something just by looking at me. To her, I'm a window, completely transparent.

We get to the harbour soon enough. The seventeenth-century plot to blow up Parliament is on our side: there is a huge firework display on at a town a few miles away and the entire local population seems to have gone.

The hulks of boats fill the water, their cables sounding like bells as they hit their masts in the wind. Reeking of fish and seaweed, it's all lobster pots and slimy ropes and buckets.

'OK.' Lorelei is pouting and arranging her hair for a selfie. I swear the girl has the attention span of an un-popped corn. 'It's called *Water Music*. He said it's written on the keel. And seriously, can we find it, because it smells absolutely vomit here.'

'From the fishing boats, do you think maybe, Einstein?' Gwenni takes gulps of air to prove that she isn't afraid of the rotting fish.

'I think this is it.' Jake has spotted it. It's small. A rowing boat with oars. It's a bit bashed about, which doesn't fill me with confidence. Neither does the inch or so of water reflecting on its floor. It has got life-jackets in it though, which makes me feel like someone knows we're using it.

'That's it? That?' Lorelei's jaw drops so far it might hit the bottom of the harbour wall. 'How are we even supposed to get into it? Jump?'

'Erm. I think we use the ladder.' Gwenni indicates the metal rungs built into the wall. 'But feel free to jump if you like.'

Not waiting for a response, she hauls herself over the drop confidently.

When she gets into the boat, we follow. Jake next, then Lorelei, me last. It's harder than it looks to climb down. The rungs are icy cold. The water slaps the last one, slippery with seaweed.

Finally, we are all in.

Lorelei holds her nose so her voice sounds like

she's swallowed helium from a balloon. 'Can we just get on with it before I throw my insides up?'

We should know better but the full moon makes us reckless. Jake picks up the oars and we plash into its reflection, shattering it into a million twinkling lights.

Chapter Seventeen

It takes a while to get any kind of rhythm going. Luckily the tide is with us and helps us to ease away from the harbour wall. We steer out through its stone mouth into the bay without anyone injuring themselves. None of us want to go too far out. Steering really isn't easy and I know we're all regretting it already.

'If you do it that way, we are just going to keep going round and round in circles.' Lorelei scowls at Jake.

'You do it then.' He thrusts an oar at her and I'm glad he has stuck up for himself for a change. Gwenni gives me a sly glance to make sure I've noticed the new lovebirds aren't getting on that well. I let her know I have.

'Eww. Not a chance. Have you actually seen my nails?'

She thrusts the oar at me and I take it. I like

dipping it into the liquid moonlight, breaking the gold into spangles, lifting them into the air. The tug of the current is strong, and it takes sheer physical effort, which starts off being a good thing, as it warms me against the cold, but quickly becomes exhausting and sweaty.

'The *Dead Eye* wreck is meant to be around here somewhere,' I remember.

'*Dead Eye* wreck? Sounds made up.'

'Actually, Jake, it's probably just named after a wooden disc they use to run ropes through. It's got three holes which look like two eyes and a nose.'

I gawp at Gwenni like her head is about to fall off.

'What? It is. I thought everyone knew that?'

I forgot that her mam used to be obsessed with swashbuckling films. Every party we had as kids, Gwenni and her mam would come dressed as pirates.

'I feel seasick.' Lorelei is so dramatic. 'Why is there no signal yet? I think I'm going to vomit chunks.'

There is a sudden sway to the water and she retches. It was pretty calm when we set out, but the wind has strengthened, so I can see why someone who doesn't have sea legs might feel a bit freaked out.

'Look. Let's just go as far as the rocks that stick up over there and then we'll give up. OK?' Gwenni highlights the rocks with her torch. 'They are called The Sirens. They used to have an iron ball on top of them to give drowning people a chance to get out of the water.'

'Wow. That's spooky.'

'But it rusted off and fell to the ocean bed.'

We all peer downwards as if we are expecting to see it.

'Apparently you can find it if you dive.'

'Jake wouldn't mind a dive, would you, Jake?' Lorelei pushes him hard and the boat rocks haphazardly.

'Seriously, Lor. What is wrong with you?' I'm scared of the deep beneath us. 'If you are going to be such a div we need to turn the boat around right now.'

I don't think I've ever called Lorelei a div before. This is an extraordinarily bad place to have a fight.

'Alright. Keep your wig on.'

She's gone back to taking photos of everything on her phone. She points her phone at the bloated moon. At the land, behind us, purple and blue. At our faces. Gwenni, lighting up the water with her torch, presumably wreck hunting; Jake sulking; me, pretending I don't know she is taking my photo, while I pose, but try not to look like I'm posing.

The wind picks up further and the temperature drops. It makes me feel uneasy, like we should turn back straight away. I ignore the instinct. 'Still no signal.' Lorelei is bitterly disappointed.

'Come on. Let's row a bit harder.'

Even here, my problems churn round in my head. I don't know how to save Snow. Is she being possessed by something dead? I wish I could ask Mam for help. Before she was ill, I could ask her anything. I long for the time when our house was filled with quarrels and shouts. Now it's all hushed voices and tiptoeing on eggshells.

A single hot tear rolls down my cheek and Gwenni elbows me to see if I'm alright. I'm not. I'm not alright at all.

'What's that?' Jake points towards the rocks. Something is there on top of them.

'O.M.G. Is it a person?'

We all lean forward. Lorelei takes a photo on her phone and enlarges it. 'Total eek. It's a seal.'

'Oh wow. I love seals.' Gwenni grins.

'Ssh. We don't want to scare it off.' I speak as quietly as I can against the wind and the sea. 'Let's get a bit closer.'

We paddle nearer, trying to dip our oars silently into the swelling waves. It's totally absorbing. If there's one thing we all have in common, it's our love of wildlife.

'So beautiful.' Lorelei is a complete animal nut. I think that's another reason why I forgive her for a lot of things.

'He's a handsome fella.'

'How do you know he's a boy?'

'No girl would be that quiet.'

'O.M.G. What's that supposed to mean?'

'It means you girls are hard work. That's what it means. You're never happy. You're always blah, blah, blahing on about stuff.'

'Is that why you wear the hat with the ear flaps?' Gwenni laughs, but the joke falls flat.

'Unfair, Jake. Totally unfair. And for that you are dumped, my friend.'

I zone out from their argument and watch as the gold coin of the moon is covered by a blood-red veil. It's an omen. I can feel something in the world switch. That's why they've started arguing. That's why the wind is getting stronger by the second. The moon is pulling us into it.

The boat rocks. The waves are increasing in size. The wind moans low and long and the boat rock-teeter-rocks.

'What's that?'

Lightning flickers on the horizon. Dad warned me how fast storms can come in here.

'I think it's a squall. We need to turn around, quick.'

'What's a squall when it's at home?' Jake doesn't seem that bothered.

'A storm. It comes in really fast. And I mean REALLY fast. We need to go back NOW.' I start rowing frantically but on my own I make no headway.

'I just want to get one more photo of the seal.'

'No. Lor. I mean now. Seriously. Or you'll be too dead to take photos.'

'Two seconds.' She stands up and I have to clutch the side of the boat to steady myself.

Ten. 'What are you thinking?'

'I don't believe it. I've got signal.' Her face lights up in the glow of her screen.

'That is so not important right now. Sit down.' Nine.

She stretches higher as messages start coming in. 'Whoop! I can't believe it. It's working.'

She jumps up and down in excitement and we all scream.

'Are you completely mad?' Start again. Ten.

'What? This?' She jumps again and laughs demonically.

'Come on. We really need to go.' Gwenni is eyeing the oncoming squall. She's right.

'I can do what I like.'

Nine. 'Are you insane? We are all going to drown.'

'I could never drown. I'm a mermaid.'

Eight. 'Sit down now, I said. Now.'

'Scared much?' She jumps again and then she's not laughing anymore, because her phone slips her grasp and makes a bid for freedom. We watch open-mouthed as it arcs up into the sky, still shining with messages, then hits the water and disappears.

'Argh! I have to get it.' She sits, finally, and starts

trying to doggy-paddle the boat towards the last sight of her phone.

'No way. It's gone. Row!' The moon is hardly visible anymore. There's just darkness and the waves are getting bigger by the second.

'I can't go without it.' Lorelei is close to tears. Jake puts his arm around her.

'Gwenni. Row. Row like you've never rowed before.'

We struggle to turn the boat to the shore, to find the red light to guide us into harbour. The waves are huge. My arms are coming out of the sockets. I wrench against the pain. We must get away from what I know is about to hit us.

It's not raining at all and then suddenly it is. Lashing down. Stinging, hard rain, like metal, like solid ice. Exhausting, drowning rain.

'Row!' I shout this to Gwenni but she can't hear me. I row hard but it's as if I'm using a matchstick. Our boat belongs to the sea. It turns side on to the waves.

Whose stupid idea was it to come out here? Lightning forks above us. If we are dragged beyond the mouth of the bay, we are dead for sure. I row but it makes no difference.

Far off I can see another firework show start and I realise there'll be no one from the town to come and save us. They'll all be looking up, while we are sinking down.

I can just make out the beach. It looks so very far away. A firework explodes above me and I watch it split into the shape of a blown dandelion clock then fall to its watery death.

The oar is almost yanked from my hands by the gobbling black sea. A bigger wave crashes over us. Cold like a million needles. The power of the water is so fierce. The world disappears for a second as panic makes me dizzy.

After all that worrying, I am going to die. And if I die then who will be there to save Snow? What was I thinking, messing about out here, leaving her alone?

I don't want to die. I concentrate on rowing hard. Harder. Focussing on the harbour. Working as a team. We make it to the harbour wall.

And then there are so many tunnels of light and hands grasping and voices. I am hauled up, out of the boat, spinning between people's hands like a runaway Catherine wheel.

Chapter Eighteen

Everyone is safe. Shaken up certainly, but alive, on solid ground. Jake is talking to the locals, who are not the least impressed with our behaviour. Lorelei is sitting silently, for once, while the boy, who apparently didn't give us permission to use his boat, has a go at her.

Gwenni is with me. 'We were so close to being knocked overboard.'

'I know.'

'We'll be in so much trouble.'

I feel like I should be crying but I'm not. I'm too worried. While I was out there on the water, who was looking out for Snow? Who was protecting her from the ghost?

'I need to go.'

'Me too.' While everyone is focussed on Lorelei and Jake, we set off as quickly as our shaky legs will carry us. I've had enough of the sea. I just want to go back, check Snow is OK, and lie down. Thunder rumbles in the distance and lightning cuts the sky far out at sea.

The moon is back and guides us intermittently through the trees to the caravans, too tired to talk, too tired to think.

'I'll see you first thing, OK?'

'I'll be too tired. But I'll see you second thing.'

I look through the window of Mam-gu's and see that she is in a deep discussion with Dad about something. Sherlock is asleep next to Marple. They must have reached some kind of truce. No sign of Mam or Snow. I wait for a few minutes just to be sure then go to ours. Mam is in bed, fast out, thank goodness, so she can't see me in this state.

'Snow.' I push into her space. There's an ever-growing pile of drawings of her and the girl in the green dress which she isn't even bothering to hide anymore. She isn't there and there's no sign of Narnia either.

The thunder rumbles more throatily than the last time. Dropping the blanket on the floor, I call for Snow again. Honestly, I could throttle her. Where on earth is she?

I strip off my wet clothes and put on a jumper and leggings. Everything hurts and I just want to go to sleep but I can't until I've found my pain of a sister. My chest is tight with fear and I can't tell if it's left over from the storm, or something else. Something yet to come.

The sky flashes bright electric white and I start counting. This time it's a mixture of anger and counting how far away the storm is.

'Snow?' I check around the caravan again in case she's in the toilet or hiding, frightened by the storm. Nothing.

Something draws me back to her room. I feel now as if I can trust my intuition. Maybe there's something in the stuff that Mam-gu always talks about. Maybe it's that I've just come really close to death.

The pictures that were piled up a second or two ago are now scattered all over the floor. My heart beats hard against my chest. Could I have created a draught when I went past them? I check over my shoulder, goose-pimples springing up all over my skin.

One of the pictures has fallen at the foot of Snow's bed. It's face down and I know somehow that it's the one I need to see. My hand trembles as I reach out and I really don't want to turn it over, but I must.

I immediately wish I hadn't.

It's the ruin but it's devastated. A fork of lightning hits its chimney. Two girls stare out from the windows with their mouths open, screaming in terror. It's drawn in angry scratched lines so violent that the paper is broken in places.

I hear a whimpering and my heart stops. Something is in the wardrobe. I can't look in there. I can't.

Summoning up all my courage, I swing the door open fast.

'Narnia!'

The puppy shoots out. I crouch down to catch her and hold her close. Looking in, I see that Snow has made a little nest for Narnia, complete with a drawing of a gaslight, like in *The Lion, the Witch and the Wardrobe*. It would be kind of cute if she hadn't left her there on her own. There must have been something really important she had to do for her to have left Narnia behind. Snow loves the dogs more than she loves any of us.

I just want to go to sleep. When is this going to

stop? I want to lie down on my bed and forget everything. But where is Snow? I can't wake Mam because she's too ill. If I go to ask Dad he'll want to know where I've been.

I can't leave it. I have to find her or I'll hate myself forever.

The sky lights up white-blue again as I tuck Narnia into my jacket. Taking a last panicked glance at the screaming girls picture, I grab the flashlight we keep by the door for emergencies and rush out into the night.

'Gwenni.' I hammer on the door and then let myself in. Charlie is running across to open it. Gwenni is behind him in her candy-floss dressing gown. Her face is streaked with tears.

'I'm sorry. You need to look after Narnia.' I give Gwenni the puppy and I'm off again, Charlie hollering after me.

I don't have time to answer. I'm running to the ruin. There's no time to be afraid now. Thunder booms so close that I think I'll be knocked down by it. I dart through the trees. It's dark in here. Too dark. Lightning flashes and the rain comes suddenly, just like it did out at sea. I don't stop. I can't stop. Boom. Closer. Even closer.

I turn the flashlight on as I run. It's raining leaves, twigs, branches, as well as water. My lungs are screeching at me and my whole body screams it can't do this. *You have to. You have to keep going.*

The ruin looms up so fast I almost run into it. I flick the beam of light around, illuminating it in pieces. It's still standing, there's no sign of any new storm damage and when I get up the courage to check, there are no screaming girls in the windows.

'Snow. Where are you?' The wind and rain are so loud they drown out my shouts. I search with the light, the lines of the trees shining back at me, leaves darting like birds, branches snapping. An enormous flicker of blue-white light and my torch catches hold of something.

I can see her. Running through the woods again like she was the day I almost went over the cliff. Like she's being chased. I can't lose her. She's my little sister. With a groan of bone against sinew, I'm running again. Trying to keep tabs on her with my flashlight.

I've lost her. Wild, I shout her name so loudly I rip the skin in my throat. *Find her, you idiot. Find her.*

Boom. The thunder shudders through me and I scream. My cry is echoed by another – *Snow.*

I run directly towards the screaming. *Where is she?*

Another flash of electric blue and I see her. Crouched in the hollow of the tree I'd spotted when I first walked here. Crouched in the place where I'd imagined a girl hiding. That can't be a coincidence. Something has brought us here.

'Snow.' I reach down and haul her out. She's screaming and screaming and screaming and screaming. I slap her across the cheek. It's a horrible thing to do, but it snaps her out of it and she focuses on me as if she is seeing me for the first time.

'We've got to go.' I pull her up to standing. She looks around as if searching for someone.

Boom. So close I drop the flashlight. Snow grabs my hand and digs her nails in so hard that I know I'm bleeding.

'No. We have to hide. They were following me,' she yells. Her voice is back with a vengeance.

'Who was following you?'

'The children. They were calling me terrible things. Dirty. Disgusting.'

'There's no one here, Snow. No one. You must have been sleepwalking.'

A whole branch of a tree hurtles past us. I grab Snow and try to drag her.

She shouts, 'I saw them. They were here. They were here.'

The rain hurts and I'm tired to death. 'We need to go back. We need to go back quickly. OK?' *Please don't start screaming again. I can't take anymore. I just can't.*

She must see something in me that tells her I'm ended. She unhooks her nails from my hand and grips it in a different way, in the way we have since forever. We run, through the tangling trees and the sucking sky. My thoughts race as fast as my feet. I see us from above, racing, and there's something so close behind. I can't make out what it is, but it's closing in, all the time, nearer and nearer, in our shadows, snatching at our heels.

Chapter Nineteen

The storm has passed, and I've slept till eleven.

When we got back last night, there was much joyful hugging and celebrating – Snow speaking, even though nobody dares ask Snow why for fear of her going quiet again — and then I was told off for leaving the caravan site without telling Dad and for going after Snow and we were made to have a warm shower and go straight to bed. I expected the fear to keep me awake but I fell straight to sleep.

Snow has slept in even later than me and I can hear her gentle snores. Mam and I have spent the last hour making collages with the sea glass, photographing each one, and listening to recorded sounds of the sea. It's supposed to be relaxing, but mostly it sounds like interference. We put up with it anyway, but quietly so that we don't wake Snow, and I'm glad that I can still make Mam laugh.

The collages are beautiful. We make a mermaid, which is a fairly obvious one, I suppose. We do a meadow scene, the sky at night and a group of dolphins. I try to make Godzilla but it looks more like a large piece of mutilated broccoli with claws. We're going to get all the photos printed into a book. Even the bad ones, Mam says.

'Just think,' Mam says, looking at a particularly beautiful piece of glass with a rose tint. 'All those lives. All those people who threw things away.'

I never really thought of them like that before: each piece having a life, or two or three, attached to it. Mam is special like that. She has an incredible ability to imagine.

'Perhaps this piece,' she holds aloft a piece of white-blue glass, 'was part of a bottle that held a message for a long-lost love.'

She sorts gently through the collection. 'And perhaps this piece…'

I am supposed to fill in the end of the sentence here. This is how Mam gets people to make up stories.

'Was a milk bottle?'

I expect Mam to laugh out loud, but she just smiles.

'And this…' She holds up a creamy green piece.

I want to do better this time, so even though I don't feel like it, I make something up.

'Was thrown into the sea by an angry…' I falter. I was about to say girl but I get a flashback of something I want to forget. '…nurse, who had sailed in a coracle across a stormy sea to save a drowning sailor, but got there just a moment too late and floundered herself on the rocks.'

Mam is well chuffed with this. I'm quite proud of it myself. Especially my use of the word 'floundered'. We pass an hour or so, Mam and me, chatting about nothing much and reminiscing. Eventually Mam wants to work. She's trying to make some money carving love-spoons and she's already sold one or two. I pack everything away, kissing my favourite pieces of sea glass for luck, and putting them at the top of the tin.

Dad is due back soon. Sherlock went with him. I think it's really to give Sherlock a rest from Narnia, who is currently crashing around chasing a ping-pong ball.

I hear Snow begin to move about next door. I'm not ready to face her. Sometimes I wish we'd never come to this unearthly place with its drowning fog and history.

'I'm popping out, Mam.'

She looks up sharply and I can tell she's wondering whether I should be wrapped up in bed and under a watchful eye for the rest of our time here. There's no way I'll be allowed anywhere if she finds out about the boat incident so I'd better make the most of my freedom while it lasts.

'I'm fine. I'm good. Honestly. If I feel anything less than amazing I promise I'll come straight back. Immediately. At once. Instantly. Promise.'

She nods. 'Remember to be careful.'

I roll my eyes and she does the same thing back, which makes me laugh. She goes straight back to her work. Carving, she looks happy. Almost well. I try not to think about cancer. I don't know it's that for sure, but people are always dying from it and she's lost weight and sleeps all the time. I can't ask. I can't form the words with my mouth.

I walk through the caravans, keeping my head down. My eyes are painful from sheer exhaustion and stress, like salt invading a cut.

I should be happy that Snow is talking again,

but I feel strange. I don't know what she meant about the children following her. All I can think is that she was sleepwalking. Or she needed to be the centre of attention. This is uncharitable of me, but my thoughts are all mixed up.

The best place to clear your mind is the beach. I don't tell Mam that's where I'm heading. I need some time alone. Distracting myself by looking for sea glass works for a while, and I find a few small glittery green and see-through pieces, but nothing of any magnificence.

Thinking about the conversation with Mam earlier, I imagine all the footsteps that have trodden this path over the years. Fishwives in scarves. Lighthouse keepers on their day off, enjoying a sandwich and the sound of the sea. Kids blowing pea-shooters to try to take out herring gulls. Women in frilly knickers being brought down to bathe in carts.

The beach is a colourful graveyard of shells. Birds fly high then drop them against the rocks to crack them and eat their fleshy insides. The smell of salt is almost visible on the air, it's so strong after last night's tumbling storm. I walk to the tide line, towards the white horses, where the seaweed changes to leaves in the water. I can just make out The Sirens, a very long way out. I feel so lucky to be alive.

Following the edge of the sea, I walk with the town and the caravans at my back. Sometimes making places smaller can make a problem seem smaller too, so I'm going to go far away and then look back on my toy-town life.

I leave No Man's Land behind, and walk the silvery path of the water, not really thinking about anything other than the beauty of my footprints, washed so quickly away. I've caught the tide as it was starting to turn out, so I have plenty of time to get back. I haven't gone beyond the dunes on this side before. Their grasses are dry and long and spiky to the touch and there are snail shells and bits of dissected crabs. I'll just climb to the top. It's not easy. The sand is soft and slips beneath each step, but I get there eventually.

It's small enough. Where I've walked. To fit into one picture. I snap it with the press of a button and then look across the far side to the world beyond the land I've claimed as mine.

The beach continues over the dune, patterned with rock pools and slivers of sand, shimmering streams and seaweed tresses. Despite my exhaustion I want to find new territory, so I half walk, half slide down and crouch on my haunches at the foot of the dune. There's a kid playing there. A small boy. He has a net and he's flinging things back into the sea. I'm too curious to ignore him, so I saunter past, taking a photo of that side of the beach so I don't look like a weirdo.

When I get closer, I can see the new beach is entirely covered in starfish. Thousands and thousands of them. All different colours, shapes and sizes.

'I'm throwing them back.' He throws one to demonstrate. 'They've been washed up by the storm and they are all dying.'

'Oh, that's very sad.'

'Some of them are dead already.' He picks up another one in his net. 'I'm only saving the orange ones.'

'Are they your favourite colour?'

'No. That's the colour they are supposed to be.'

I don't know what to say to this. I gaze out at the horizon. 'Don't you think that the starfish might not be able to choose what colour they are when they are born?'

The boy visibly thinks about it. He scratches his head. 'You're brown.'

'I am.'

'My friend Sam is brown.'

'Is he?'

He falls about in fits of laughter. 'Sam's a girl.'

'Oh. Sorry.' He picks up a different-coloured starfish and throws it back into the sea. Then another and another. All colours. All of them. I join in and help by scooping them up with plenty of sand under them in case they can sting my hands.

'I think that one was dead already.' He points at one which has washed back up.

'We can only try our best. Keep up the good work.'

I have to go because someone is walking towards us and I'm guessing she's the boy's mother. I can't face any confrontation today.

I make the long trek back in a kind of haze and plonk myself down on the sand close to the stream to rest.

Snow comes to sit by me. I know it's her before I even look. She smells of bluebells and playdough and sister. I don't know what to say to her. I feel nervous, like I'm not sure who she is.

'She'll tell you why, if you like? She says you want to know, so she'll tell you.'

'Who will?'

'The girl. She'll tell you why she's here.'

I look at her. She has tiny snowflake impressions on her face where she's slept with her hand against her cheek. She has a snowflake ring and I have birds. Mam had them cast in silver, copper and gold especially for us.

'OK.'

'You have to turn away.'

I turn away.

'And put your hands over your eyes.'

For once I don't argue. Usually I would tell her to sod off. Today I put my hands over my eyes.

'Go on. Don't be scared. Tell her why you were here.'

Snow acts like she is talking to someone. I am about to look when I feel a cold sensation at the back of my neck, like a cloud has passed over the sun or when someone reveals your deepest secret, which they had promised to keep.

'I saw the planes coming in.' It's not Snow's voice. It's different. An accent I don't recognise. The voice sounds unused, unsure.

'Go on.' Snow's voice. 'Don't look, Lark. Promise.'

I nod, my hands clasped firmly over my eyes. A sweat has broken out on my forehead and I want to look so badly. So, so badly.

'The children, they were chasing me, and I hid in the crook of a tree.'

I wait. I want to open my eyes and find Snow putting on a voice. But what if I don't? What if she isn't alone?

'I saw the planes coming and I was running to tell my mother.'

The accent. It's German. I've heard it in films.

'And then the sky was so much fire. The sky of fire, then nothing.'

'I think I understand.' I don't know how I manage to speak. I don't understand at all, but I do want her, whoever or whatever she is, to go on. To get to the end of her story so that she can leave us alone.

'I am collecting the pretty glass from the beach to put the windows back together. When it is nice, my mother will come back for me. She likes things to be tidy and clean to show people we are nice and not bad.'

Snow's own voice takes over, as if she is talking to someone younger. 'Your mother will find you.

You have to be brave now. You have to go. It's time for you to leave. I'll miss you. But I have to spend time with my real family now.'

There's a feeling of lightness inside me and a breath close to my ear.

'You can open your eyes. She's gone.'

The light is bright and twinkles from the stream and the sea.

'She was just lonely. The ghost wanted someone to play with. She didn't realise that you could hurt yourself if you fell from a cliff or kill a bird if you squeezed it too tight.'

We look into each other, Snow and me.

'Is she really gone?'

'Yes.' We both smile.

'I'm glad you're talking again, Snow.'

'Me too. I needed you to rescue me. So I had to shout.'

'I'll always find you when you need me.'

'I know.'

She goes to squash my face like it's been stuck in a lift again. This time I get there first.

Chapter Twenty

Time has stopped. The sky is pressing down. I've lost my temper big time. One of the cupboard doors in the kitchen hangs by its hinges and smashed crockery covers the floor. I've damaged things and they're not even ours.

'Why don't you ask her?' I point at Mam. I have never been this rude to her in my life.

'Don't talk to your mam that way.' Dad is shocked by the way I'm behaving but I don't care. I can't hold it in anymore. I had thought things were calming down. The girl is gone and Snow is talking and we should have been happy.

But then Mam got cross and ordered me not to go near the beach again, she'd found out about us going out in the boat. Told me that I might have died, had a real go at me, shouted and looked disappointed. And all that stuff that's been bubbling up deep inside me burst out in boiling screams of anger.

I kick the wall in frustration.

'Lark.'

Mam has her black dress on, her hair is tied up scruffily, her mascara is clogged and she has tears in her eyes.

I kick the door again and then hit it with my fists.

'What is it, Lark?'

'You know what it is. Don't pretend you don't.'

'I don't, sweetheart, but if you tell me we can work it out together.'

Yeah. Like we can work out how to stop her from dying.

'It's you.'

When the words come I can't stop them and I say it over and over again. 'It's you. You. You. You.'

I'm snarling and spitting like a cornered wild animal. Dad is holding me around the waist, but I don't stop. Mam comes over and grabs my hands so I can't hurt myself. Finally, we crumple to the floor.

'Right now, Lark. Firstly, calm down. Ten... Nine...'

I breathe fast and make all the noises of crying but there's still no tears. Mam's voice comes to me from a far-off place even though she's right next to me.

'What do you mean, *it's you*?'

My jaw aches as I speak. 'I know you are going to die.'

There. It's out. The pain of saying it out loud fills the air and hammers into the ground.

'Everyone is going to die, Lark.'

'But not now. You're dying now.'

I howl from deep, deep, deep inside. From a place where I've never been before. The darkest place in the universe.

'Lark. I'm not dying. What are you talking about? Lark? Lark?' Mam slaps my face. I deserve that. I did it to Snow.

'You said,' I accuse her. 'You've been crying and sleeping all the time and…'

'Oh, Lark. No.'

'I heard you through the wall. You said to Dad that you were dying. *I'm dying here*, you said. *I'm dying here*. You. Said.'

'Lark. I said that — that's why we came on holiday. To the sea. I needed a break to be able to breathe. I needed a break from life back home. For my anxiety. For my depression, Lark. Not because I'm dying.'

Dad is still holding me, and Mam is crying, and

now I am crying, and the tears are so hot and so painful.

'I'm not dying, Lark.'

Dad rubs my back. 'Your mam was having problems with feeling unhappy, no, more than unhappy, despair, but she is getting better now, and she is learning to share her feelings and getting help.'

Somewhere in my head a light goes on. I start to let this sink in.

'It was a stupid thing to say that I was dying. And you weren't meant to hear that, Lark. It's just I felt so awful. So hopeless. I used the wrong words. I'm sorry.'

They taught us a bit about depression in school. That's why Mam finds it difficult to meet new people and go into shops. That explains the weight loss and the heavy sleeps. The crying and panics and dark, sad days. It fits together — now that I know what it is.

'Why are you depressed?' I'm so afraid to ask the next question but I have to know the answer. 'Is it because of me?'

'What?' Mam wipes her tears away.

'Is it because I get so angry all the time?'

'Of course, it's not because of you. You are the best daughter anyone could wish for.'

'Your mam is ill, Lark. But she's getting better and that's the important thing.'

'And part of that is because of you, my sweet, beautiful, clever, headstrong daughter.' Mam hugs me close. I let her.

Our hug is broken by a small furry ball hurtling its way into the caravan followed closely by an exhausted-looking Sherlock who immediately goes to his bed and lies down.

'Guess what?' Snow's face is glowing from the cold outside. She stops, framed by the doorway. 'What's going on?'

'Nothing.' Dad goes and fills the kettle like nothing has happened here.

My face burns.

'We were just having a chat.'

Snow looks at us on the floor. The cupboard door hanging. The state of me and Mam.

I clear my throat. I am going to have to tell her I was wrong. I am going to have to admit to what I told her, in front of Mam and Dad.

She stares at us for a second, waiting for someone to tell her the truth.

My words stick in my throat like a lump of scorching coal.

'Well, whatever it is, you have to come and look.'

She beckons us to the door. We look out to see snowflakes falling. Like sequins swirling in the air. Mam, Dad and Snow are out in it in seconds, letting it land in their hands and watching it melt, wearing snow crowns of it, catching it on their tongues, laughing. Narnia puts two tiny paws out and then turns back. Sherlock plods out and then becomes a frolicking pup again.

I stand inside the door and watch them. I want to go out and join the fun, but how can I after what I've done to Snow? I don't deserve to.

She sees me watching and comes back to grab my hand. 'Come on. What's wrong with you? You're missing it.'

'Mam's not dying.'

She drops my hand. 'What?'

'You heard me.'

'What do you mean?'

'What do you think I mean? Are you stupid or something?'

'But you said.'

'I got it wrong. It's depression. She has depression.'

'But you said she was dying.'

'That's what she said. But I got it wrong, OK? I didn't understand. How many times?'

She takes a step towards me. I hope she'll squash my face like it's been stuck in a lift. She doesn't. She steps back then turns and runs, straight past Mam and Dad. Into the woods.

Chapter Twenty-One

Snow hasn't spoken to me since yesterday and now she is avoiding me. Everyone is making the most of the snow before it melts. Despite everyone saying that it was a freak weather occurrence brought to us straight from Siberia and that there was no way it would stick, it has stuck and they are all snowball fighting and building snow people and the smallest igloos which collapse every five minutes. We knew it would be a cold holiday but none of us had even dreamed of snow. It's like some kind of miracle and we are all hoping that it means going back home to school will be cancelled.

Mam is inside, whittling a spoon and I want to help out, so I offer to make all the beds. Mam gets up straight away and feels the temperature of my forehead and then collapses in stitches. She's not well, but she's here, and once you face your fear you can deal with it, whatever that fear is.

The guilt of traumatising my little sister makes me restless, so having a task is almost welcome. Mam and Dad's bedroom is tiny and I'm sweaty and pretty annoyed by the time I manage to get it all straight. I almost don't bother with Snow's bed, but the guilt reminds me I have to.

I decide to give her clean covers. We brought spares. She's got her baby-blue cover on. It's her favourite so it'll probably be on again as soon as it's out of the wash when we get home. For now, I'm going to put on one that's covered with stars. I tussle with the blue cover and as it finally gives in and lets itself be removed, something falls to the floor.

It's a very small piece of sea glass. Nothing unusual in that, we've had the stuff all over the place, but it makes me stop to think. I check where everyone is. Snow is out with the other kids, Mam is working, Dad is putting the teeth on a pathetically small snowman. I know it's not right to poke around in someone else's things, but I reason that I'm doing it for Snow's safety. It's a poor excuse but I'll use it all the same.

There's nothing else inside her duvet cover. I check it twice in case something has got stuck in the folds. There's nothing under the mattress, under the bed, behind the curtains, in her wardrobe. There's nothing anywhere.

I'm relieved, of course, but there's also something niggling away at me. Where's that hideous doll? I wipe the condensation from the window and look out, then almost jump a mile when I see that Snow has stopped, frozen in the centre of the mayhem, and is staring straight at me.

'I'm changing your duvet,' I mouth and then hold up the dirty one to show her. She doesn't react. She's not stupid. She glances across to Mam-gu's caravan. It's an almost imperceptible glance but if you've known someone your whole life you would notice it. She smiles at me fake innocently then goes back to climbing the small snowy bank, so she can sledge down it on a tea-tray. I look as if I'm taking my time tidying. Make a show of picking up the duvet cover and a sock from the floor. I go back in to Mam.

'I'm nearly done.' Mam's tongue pokes out like Snow's does when she's concentrating. A lamp on the table is focused directly on a symbol that she's carving, and she's lost in the pool of light. I don't want to disturb her when she's so involved in her work, so I sneak out quietly.

Of course, I'm hit by a snowball to the face immediately and I give Jake a look that tells him I'm not at all impressed. I can't see where Snow has gone. I scan round as quickly as I can. Jake is shoving snow down the back of Lorelei's collar. Gwenni and Charlie are concentrating on the doorway to their half-collapsed igloo. Wiley Riley is scattering seeds for the birds. No sign of Snow.

I go to Mam-gu's caravan. Snow's in there sitting on Mam-gu's chair. I can see how angry she still is with me. I'm not scared of my own sister. I'm not.

'Why aren't you out there playing with all the others?'

'Why aren't you?'

'Because I'm thirteen.'

'So?'

'So I don't play.'

'That's sad.'

She's right. It is sad but not in the way she means it. I look around as if I'm just hanging out here and taking in my surroundings casually. Someone clatters up the steps. It's two life-savers in the form of Leila-J and Betsey-Anne. 'Snow, come and see the snow sculpture we've made.'

'It's amazing. It's in the shape of a throne and we can all sit on it like royalty.'

'We're having our photo taken in it.'

'Come on, before the arms fall off.'

They grab Snow, who gives me a wrathful glower, then leaves with them. I know that as soon as that photo is taken she'll be back. The place is small enough so if there's anything here it shouldn't be hard to find. I shut the door, when I've checked that Snow is well away.

It's almost too easy. There's a bucket in the cupboard under the sink with a bin bag in it, which would convince anyone else that it was being used for rubbish, but I know better. *Nice try, Snow. I'm impressed.*

Glancing over my shoulder, I fish it out and untie it, trying desperately not to tear the plastic so I don't leave any signs of breaking and entering.

The doll is the first thing I see but instead of the old blank sockets it now has new, painted on eyes. Snow is a brilliant artist and I have to put the doll face down, so she doesn't follow my every movement. There's a load of sea glass in a smaller plastic bag and then right at the bottom a stack of leaflets held together with an elastic band.

A snowball hits the wall of the caravan outside and I feel the bones of my skeleton jolt. I listen and hold my breath. Shrieks of laughter, one of the kids crying, the muffled thud of snowballs hitting other things.

I pull the leaflets out. They are the usual collection of local interest things that you get pretty much everywhere. A model village that looks about a hundred years old, a steam train that chuffs its way along the side of a verdant hill, an impressive waterfall that I decide immediately I am going to go and see. I leaf through them rapidly. They must be things that Snow has been copying for her drawings. There must be something else. I check the bin bag again and right at the bottom of the bucket, in case I've missed anything. I start to put things back in the bag and a leaflet which had been hidden inside another, flutters down and lands on my knees.

Local Myths & Legends. I check over my shoulder. It's a good job I can read fast. It's the usual sort of stuff. Dragons, changelings coming in from the sea, petrified forests, the witches who lived in the woods and on the back the story of the German ghost. A girl who was killed tragically with her mother in a night of the Blitz. The Luftwaffe caught their house in the woods with a bomb, in a night of terror so horrific that the sky seemed to be on fire. How she is said to appear, in the green dress she wore that day, to wreak her revenge.

Snow has known this story all along.

I'm sweating. I check over my shoulder again. And then again.

She and her mother were living in a rundown house in the woods. They'd been ostracised from the community because of their nationality. The girl's father had been arrested and taken away as a prisoner of war, even though he'd come here as a refugee.

I place all the leaflets carefully back in the exact order they were before, trying not to look the doll in the face. Tying the knot in the same way I place the bucket back. As I spin the bucket a couple of centimetres to the left, I dislodge something else.

It's Mam-gu's photo album. Why has Snow hidden this? I open it and one of the pictures is loose.

It's a very old photo I can't remember Mam-gu showing us. It's black & white, gone a bit brown with age, and faded at the edges. I tilt it to pick up the blue-white snowy light from outside, so I can see it properly. It only takes me a split second to work out who the girl in the photograph is. It's my mam-gu; I've seen pictures of her at this young age before. She's outside somewhere, smiling directly into the camera. She looks so happy. Behind her there's a line of washing caught forever in the wind. And then I see something that makes my head spin so fast my brain hurts. Behind the washing, in the woods, there's a figure. Hard to distinguish because of the quality of the photograph, but I know her. I hold it up closer to my face. My mind is racing, and my mouth is as dry as a desert. The figure is grainy, blurred, but I'm almost completely certain it's the German girl.

'What are you doing?'

'Oh for…' I drop the photo and snatch it back up. 'You scared me half to death.'

'Why have you got all my stuff out?' Snow's face is glowing from the cold and fury.

'Why have you hidden it in here?'

'I haven't hidden it, dweeb face. There's no room in our caravan in case you hadn't noticed.'

I have a moment of doubt. 'Oh yeah. Then why did you put it in a bag?'

'Erm, because you've been trying to make me get rid of the doll since I found it, so I knew you wouldn't want to see it.'

'Oh. OK. Well, there's no need to be ratty about it.'

'I'm not. Just leave my stuff alone.'

I slide the photograph into my back pocket as she takes her bag out from under the sink to check I haven't messed with her stuff.

'The ghost is back again, isn't she?'

She stops, for such a minuscule amount of time it's almost unnoticeable, and then carries on. 'What do you mean?'

'You've brought all this stuff over here to show her, haven't you?'

'You're crazy.'

'OK. Maybe I am. But you are still talking to her, aren't you? Why else would you hide all this stuff over here? It's her doll, isn't it?'

'If you like.'

'No, I don't like. It's the truth.'

'What would you know about the truth? You told me Mam was dying.'

I stagger. 'I apologised. I made a mistake. What do you want me to do, grovel?'

'Maybe. It's going to take me a lifetime to get over it.'

'It's going to take me a lifetime to get rid of the guilt. Satisfied?'

'Good. I'm glad. I hope you feel guilty forever.' She picks up a cushion and throws it at me. The zip catches the corner of my eye and really hurts.

I yell a battle cry as I run towards her.

'Enough!' Mam-gu never ever shouts. She completely fills the caravan doorway with her presence and we are blown apart by her holler but I still want to retaliate so I keep on yelling.

'I said, that's enough.'

I don't ignore her twice. I reach into my back pocket instead and hold the photograph up to her.

'And you,' I say. 'Enough hiding.'

Chapter Twenty-Two

'It's time to put this to rest.' Mam-gu's eyes are watery and her voice quakes.

We wait. We can tell there's something important coming. I'm not sure we want to hear it.

Mam-gu sits with difficulty on her chair. 'She was my friend.'

'Who? The German girl?' This is out of my mouth without thought.

'She had a name. Erika. She was my best friend.'

Snow sits at Mam-gu's feet. I don't want to join the cosiness of this gathering.

'She was such a funny girl. And brave too. Braver than I've ever been.' She gets lost for a moment then comes back to her story.

'What happened, Mam-gu?' Snow puts her hand gently on Mam-gu's knee.

'I had no friends when I lived here.'

'Here?'

'Don't interrupt. I need to get to the end of this. I found it difficult. I was shy and different. Your mother was the same when she was young. The other children, they used to bully me for being quiet. It made me an easy victim. I used to come to the woods to play alone. There were silly rumours about witches living here. Most of the local children believed it, so I knew I'd be away from them. I remember hearing her singing. I was collecting daisies and this voice, so pure and clear, threaded its way like ribbon through the trees. I swear she enchanted me.' Mam-gu smiles.

We say nothing.

'She spoke English. With a strong accent, yes. But good. At first she tried to run from me but I sat right down and started singing and making a daisy chain. She came back. I don't think anyone ever started a fight by making a daisy chain.'

We don't move.

'We were friends. We looked out for each other.' She eyes us both and I squirm, knowing that she means me and Snow should be kinder to each other and to everyone else. 'We did everything together. So much fun. Until…'

'Go on.' My heart is thumping against my chest.

'I said, don't interrupt.' She rearranges herself and Snow clasps hold of her hand tightly. 'That day, it was bright. So beautifully hot and sunny. The sky was blue and the sea. Like a sapphire. We couldn't resist the beach. We'd been warned of the dangers, of course, but we were children. We just wanted to play on the sand. To be free.'

I feel hot. Afraid.

'They found us playing there, the others from school. I bet they couldn't believe their luck to find us together. Like two birds with one stone.'

A crow *cwaraks* outside.

'I tried to talk to them, but they were set on something else. There was a gang of them. Only us two.' Her chest heaves and she prises her hand away from Snow. 'They hit me first. They were going to hit her. I threw sand up in their faces.'

She demonstrates with air.

'And we ran. The two of us. Into the woods. We thought we could escape them. They caught me first.'

It's hard to see Mam-gu like this. I've never seen her struggle before. I wish I could stop her but I have to know what happened. She needs to say it.

'I was scared. Terrified. I thought they were

going to kill me. I don't know. I knew where she would be hiding. I told them. They surrounded her, called her awful things. Horrible things. And I just stood there. Petrified. As if I was one of them. I betrayed her.'

Mam-gu rubs at the scar on her head.

My palms sweat even though it's freezing. 'You were young.'

'I knew what was right and wrong.'

'You were scared.'

'It's no excuse.' Mam-gu looks like an unstrung puppet. I want to run to her and hug her, but there's something inside me that is angry, too.

'That same night the bombs came. We were lucky to survive. Others weren't so lucky.'

She stares out of the window.

'I never got to say sorry.' She is so forlorn but I have to ask.

'Why would you bring us here? It's dangerous.'

She laughs. 'There's no danger here. She's just a little girl and I need to put things right.'

The wind roars. It is darker, as if the day has been put out. Snow looks over her shoulder sharply.

'What is it?' Mam-gu staggers to standing.

'She's here.' Snow stands too.

'You don't need to be afraid. She's not dangerous at all.'

I feel suddenly on fire.

'I need to tell her I'm sorry.'

Snow looks to the side of me. I'm burning up. It's as if a thousand matches have been struck against my skin.

'She says she trusted you.' Snow's eyes are like saucers.

'I don't know what to say. I'm so sorry.' Tears stream down Mam-gu's face.

'She says she thought you were her friend.'

I can't swallow. The heat is so intense. It's constricting my airwaves. Sweat pours from my brow and I feel so woozy, so dizzy.

'She says you took everything from her.' Snow looks so scared. 'She's so angry. I've never seen her like this.'

I claw at my throat to get my jumper away from it. Why is it so blisteringly hot?

'Oh Mam-gu. She's SO angry.'

I turn and she's there. Right next to me. An inch away. So small. So real.

The girl turns and holds her hand out to Snow. I don't know what to do. I can't breathe properly.

'It's fine, Mam-gu. She just wants a friend.' Snow reaches out towards the girl.

'No. She needs to go now. It's time for you to go.' Mam-gu is trying to get to Snow before she reaches the girl. I don't think she can see her but I can tell from Mam-gu's face that she is afraid.

'It's OK. I'm going to go with her. She just wants someone to be close.'

Snow reaches her hand out to the girl and I snap back to reality. My sister needs me.

I throw myself in front of Snow, pushing her back towards Mam-gu. 'Leave her alone.'

The girl's eyes glitter with rage.

'You have to go away and leave us all alone.' I'm shouting because I'm scared of what will happen to Snow. I'm shouting because this is the freakiest, scariest thing imaginable. 'Go away and leave us all alone.'

I rush at the girl headlong and suddenly there is nothing but flames and stars and I'm in excruciating pain. I can't see anything. I'm blinded. As if the world is on fire and I am screaming. Screaming.

Chapter Twenty-Three

Mam's face has drained of blood. 'That's a terrible story.'

She pats my forehead with a cool cloth and I try to put those terrible images out of my mind.

'The Germans were the ones who did the bad things. To everyone.' My voice is tight, tight, tight in my throat. 'Everyone says it.'

Everyone says it except Mam-gu. I feel sick at what I've seen. How bad must she feel carrying it with her throughout most of her life?

I think of Mam-gu saying she deserved the scar on her forehead for betraying a friend, and without wanting to I replay everything I saw in the fire. The girl cowering, the mob chasing, the stone hitting my Mam-gu in slow motion, splitting the skin, causing a scar that would never heal.

'I didn't know you would be in danger. I just

wanted to come here to put things right.' Mam-gu who would never talk about her life here. Mam-gu who made up glittering stories to cover the truth.

'Most of the German people were just normal people going about their lives. That's what war is. Isn't it?' Mam scratches at the surface of the table with her thumbnail as she thinks. I feel my face burn at the thought of doing to others what some people do to us. Grouping us together. Pointing a finger. Fear is a horrible thing. Look what it did to Mam-gu. Look what it is doing to me.

We have gathered around Mam-gu's table, the four of us. Snow looks exhausted. Mam-gu has new white streaks in her hair which have appeared overnight. I haven't looked at myself. I'm afraid of what I'll see.

Gwenni walks past the window and I bang the glass to get her to come in.

'What's happened?'

She can tell it's something serious from our faces.

'The ghost thing. Still here. Seen her. Properly this time.'

'Oh. Wow.' She pops her gum. 'So, what now?'

'We are deciding how to get rid of her.' I feel bad for my choice of words. 'How to convince her to go to where she belongs.'

'OK.' Gwenni sits.

'I guess that's five of us then.'

Mam has Snow *cwtched* right up to her. Mam-gu is in bits. I have to be strong. 'There's strength in numbers.'

I spot familiar ear flaps and pink hair through the window. 'I'll be right back.'

Gwenni groans, but they've been part of it almost since the beginning so it seems right they'll be part of the end. Whatever the end is going to be.

I call Lorelei and Jake over and wait till they get right up to me so no one can overhear. 'The ghost is real.'

'No way.'

'Way.' I take a deep breath. It seems surreal even now.

For all their annoyingness I'm glad they are going to be involved.

Inside, Mam scooches up so there is room on the bench. We huddle around the table.

'How does this work then?' Jake looks more scared than any of us.

'We need to persuade her she'll be happier when she isn't tied to this place.' I've appointed myself spokesperson because Mam-gu looks awful and everyone else looks lost. 'When we saw her she was really angry. It might take a bit of persuasion.'

We make a plan and decide to meet when night falls so no one else sees us and wants to come along. It's better to keep it to those who already know and understand.

'I'll see you later.' I wave goodbye to everyone. I need some time alone to process things. Mam told me that the brain is a complicated organ that can sometimes get overloaded. It's OK to not cope. It's OK to need time to work things out.

Chapter Twenty-Four

The day goes too fast and bleeds into night too soon.

I give Snow a full-on bear hug. I've learned how to do it from Dad.

'I can't breathe.'

She squirms out of my arms.

'Put this on.' I give her my favourite red jumper, picking off a couple of bobbles where it's worn. I don't know if I'm going to be able to protect her tonight, but I can at least make sure she's warm. Mam clatters about. It's funny, in this crisis she seems more alive than ever. She's told Dad we are going bat-watching. It's not exactly a lie as we might happen to see some bats. Dad's not a fan of them. We are due to go home tomorrow. We are back at school on Tuesday. We could leave, but it would feel like running, like Mam-gu did before. It doesn't feel right to leave without trying to help, for Mam-gu or for Snow. Or for Erika.

Snow hooks her thumbs through the holes I've made. 'It looks better on you. You can have it.'

She comes over and hugs me thank you, then steps away quickly before I crush her again. Mam is waiting for us, twiddling her hair around her fingers and trying to look 'normal' for Dad's sake. There's no need. His head is stuck in a book and I can tell from his face that he is lost in that world.

'We're off, Dad.' I stem the urge to give him a hug too. He'll know there's something fishy if I do.

'See you later. Look after each other.' He goes back to reading, hardly glancing up.

'We will.'

We're meeting at the ruin. We don't want to gather nosy stragglers along the way.

Using torches to guide us through the trees, we tread carefully so we don't fall over roots on the uneven ground. I'm leading. Mam and Snow hold hands behind. Snow was chitter-chatting non-stop when we left – I think she's making up for lost time. As we draw close to the ruin, she falls silent.

Mam-gu is here already with Gwenni. Gwenni was too scared to come alone.

'Hi.' Words sound strange. 'You both OK?'

'As good as we'll ever be.' Gwenni speaks gravely and Mam-gu's face mirrors her tone.

Jake and Lorelei arrive.

I look around my motley crew and my heart swells with love to the point of pain. This needs to be done. It needs to be over. 'Here goes nothing.'

'Here goes...'

'Please don't say "everything", Jake. We aren't in some pants American tween movie.' Lorelei must be taking this mortally seriously because she spends her entire life trying to pretend she is one of the girls from these films. Perhaps she is growing a brain now that she no longer has a phone.

'We need to go in.' I pull the brambles back for everyone, pricking my thumbs and almost swearing before I remember that Mam and Mam-gu are here. We gather at the centre of the ruin.

Mam-gu holds up candles and Mam lights them one by one with the shivering flame of a lighter. We put them around us, everywhere – in the crevices, on the ground, chasing the shadows out.

'What do we do now?' I'm staying close to Snow so I can mind out for her.

'I need to apologise properly.' Mam-gu looks around her. 'For what I did. And explain why I did it. I think that's the first step.' She puts her hands out with her palms up to the air as if she is waiting to catch something. 'Erika. I'm sorry. I'm sorry for what I did. It's not enough. I know. I was scared. So scared and…'

When she pauses, I go towards her because I want to help. It's awful to see Mam-gu in so much pain. She signals me to stay away.

'I've carried it all my life. What I did. It's no excuse. But it's the truth and it's all I have to offer.'

I expect some kind of banshee howling, or a gust of wind. Nothing. The night is perfectly still. An owl screeches above. Something scuttles in the corner, a hedgehog or a rat. 'Why isn't she coming?'

Snow shrugs. 'I don't know.'

'She's been following you around for ages. You must have some idea.'

'She was so angry last time. I think she must be upset and hiding.'

'OK. So how do we coax her out?'

Snow shrugs again.

'Anyone got any bright ideas? We have got to end this *now*.' I simply can't take any more.

There's no answer from anyone.

'Aren't we supposed to stand in a circle or something?' Jake keeps laughing as if it will make him appear less terrified.

'We might as well try it.' As we can't think of anything else.

'It's alright, Jake. There's nothing to be frightened of.' Snow links arms with him. We follow suit and all link arms so we are in a ring.

'What should we do, Mam-gu?'

Mam-gu looks so old and unsure. She shakes her head. 'I have no idea.'

'But you said to me, before, you said you have to go and help that girl. You knew she was here.'

'Of course I knew she was here. Why do you think we came back? I need to put it right. But I don't know how, any more than any of you do.'

'You picked the perfect time to tell us that.'

'Shut up, Lorelei.' I turn back to Mam-gu. 'Why did you tell me that I had to help her?'

'Because I could tell from your face that you'd seen her. Snow, she is too young. You are so strong. Such a courageous girl. Erika wouldn't appear to me as I got old. I've been back here many times. I've tried. I suppose she doesn't know who I am anymore. I didn't know she was dangerous. She was just a little girl.' Mam-gu looks tired to death. 'I should never have expected it of you. It's too much.'

'You didn't have a choice.' I grasp her shoulders. 'Like you said. It has to be put right.'

'Thank you.'

I look at everyone's faces. Someone has to think of something. Someone has to sort this whole thing out. 'She said she was collecting sea glass. To make the windows whole.'

'What are you on about?'

'Shut up, Lor. Snow, have you got any?'

Snow shakes her head.

'Damn. I should have thought. It brought her out last time.' I think back to that first day on the beach. The day I first saw her. I was wearing these jeans. I check my pockets. They've been through the wash, surely not…

And yet there it is, that first innocent piece of sea glass. It's hardly anything at all, but the smallest things can have enormous power. I place it in the centre of our circle. 'Shine your torches on it.'

Everyone does, but not before I catch Gwenni's baffled look and the glance which passes between Jake and Lorelei.

Nothing happens.

'Nothing's happening.'

'Thanks for stating the obvious, Jake.'

'Shut up, Lorelei.' That's Mam this time. She never tells people to shut up unless they are really getting on her last nerve.

Jake's right though. Nothing is happening.

'Why isn't it working?' I'm desperate. 'Snow, she's been following you around the whole time. Why isn't she here now?'

All I get is an awkward shrug.

'Mam-gu, you said you were singing.' It's another ridiculous idea but I can't think of anything else. 'That day she came back. You were singing a song and making a chain from some flowers.'

I wish we had flowers here now. 'What was the song? It's OK if you can't remember.'

'Of course I can remember. That day is imprinted on my mind as if it were yesterday.'

'We could make a chain from these. I brought them just in case.' Gwenni holds out the snowflakes from Snow's coat. 'They are a bit like flowers.'

She sounds so doubtful but it's perfect.

'We are going to re-enact it, Mam-gu. I know you've kept it all to yourself for so long, but you have to let it go now.'

'OK.'

It's a long shot but it's all we've got.

We link arms again around Mam-gu. We shine our torch beams at her and the sea glass and as she places the snowflakes in a pattern she begins to sing in her old tongue. The Welsh she used as a child that we all learn now in school.

'I know this one.' Jake starts to join in.

'Ssh. You don't want to scare her away.' Gwenni tells him off.

'Ssh, both of you. It needs to just be Mam-gu.'

Her voice sounds so strange here in the carcass of the house at the dead of night. It seems a miracle that she can sing at all, but she continues, looking to us to reassure her that she is doing the right thing. It has to work. It has to.

Mam-gu's voice sings out its reedy refrain into the darkness and from the darkness another voice joins in.

Chapter Twenty-Five

'Keep singing, Mam-gu.' Our eyes dart about the ruin. It's what we wanted, but the reality of it is still terrifying. 'Don't be afraid.' I call this out into the shadows beyond the candlelight. 'We won't hurt you.'

The voice is hesitant at first. The girl sings along with Mam-gu. I guess she learned the language enough back then, when they were friends.

The end of the song comes too soon and with the last note Mam-gu seems to shrink. She pulls herself together and holds the piece of sea glass up to catch the beams of the torches. From nowhere the girl appears in the centre of the circle, next to her. She's not solid. She's more of an impression, flittering in and out of focus as if she is a fading memory. It's hard to describe.

Mam-gu swallows, opens her mouth to speak,

but can't. Someone has to say something, before the moment is lost.

'Tell us what you want from us.' I sound stronger than I feel.

'She's sorry.' Snow is speaking for the girl as if she understands her by telepathy. 'She doesn't want to be alone any longer.'

The girl turns and faces me. I balk. My mouth opens and shuts like a goldfish gasping for air. The burning sensation starts again, constricts my breathing. It is like two burning hands around my throat. I have got to keep it together.

'She's sorry but she wants a friend and you are getting in the way, Lark.'

I'm burning to a frazzle but no one seems to notice. They are all transfixed by the girl. She is staring at me. I can't bear the heat. Sweat pours out of me like lava.

'I can't … breathe.' My throat is getting so tight. I can't get any air. 'Please…'

I'm asking the girl to stop the pain. It's directed only at me and it's searing. She is coming closer and as she does her anger burns into my flesh. I can't take any more. I'm going to die if I stay here.

I let go and run. Straight out through the

cutting brambles and into the thick woods. I can hear them shouting behind me but I keep going. Their cries holler through the woods, echoing in my wake. The shouts are caught up by the wind and chase me through the trees. They are too close. I can't run any faster. I can't escape.

My lungs are exploding. Stars of pain dazzle me. I have to stop. To catch my breath. I crouch inside the hollow of a tree. Their voices are far off, like something underwater. I huddle down, making myself as small as I can. Stay calm. I breathe in short rasps. I try to slow my breathing down, to concentrate on getting oxygen deep into my lungs.

The heat is dying down a bit. Breathe. I can still hear their voices. Far away, calling my name over and over. People will hear. Dad won't think we are bat watching now.

There's a sulphurous feeling at the back of my nose which spreads rapidly to my throat. She's close. She's found me. I can feel her anger strangling me. I scrabble blindly about in the belly of the tree, find a stone and hurl it blindly into the darkness. And then I run again.

I should go back. I should protect Snow and

Mam, Mam-gu and the gang. I'm too afraid. I'm such a coward.

I burst from the woods. In the sparse light of the moon, I see the thundering sea, the beach and look down on the rocks at the bottom of the cliff where I came out before.

I know there is a path down to the beach, but I've dropped my torch so I'll be lucky to get down it alive. I have to try, though. I can't stay here like prey, waiting at the edge of the cliff for the girl to come and push me over. I can't go back into the woods. I'm just too scared. The voices have died away. I'm all alone out here. No. No. Not entirely alone.

Finding the top of the path isn't easy and once I've found it I know that I'm taking my life in my hands. I could sit and wait it out till morning, but something tells me that I wouldn't make it till the sun rose. I'd die of exposure, if nothing else. There's no fog this evening but the clouds are scudding through the sky and the cold snatches my breath.

I use the wavering moonlight to make my way down. Scree skids under my boots and rattles down the path ahead of me. I can't think about falling. I have to keep moving.

I get to the beach, panting for breath, a stitch stabbing my side. I can make my way across the sand back from here. If I can see enough not to slide and fall on the icy rocks.

She's still with me. There's a snicker of a laugh close to my ear.

'What do you want from me?' I need to face my fears. 'Tell me.'

I can't see her. The wind blows hard in from the sea. I have nothing to lose. 'Stop being such a coward. Come on. Face me. I dare you.'

'I am not a coward.'

She's there. Right in front of me. Fading in and out. Her eyes glittering. Her fury scalds.

'Why are you trying to hurt me?' The wind hurls my voice at her. 'You are not taking my sister.'

She is blisteringly livid. Her shouts cut straight into my brain. 'I won't be alone anymore.'

'I won't let you have her.' The sea is so close. 'You'll have to drown me first.' I run. But not away. This time I run straight at her. Facing my fear head on. She cowers down and I laugh spitefully. 'Afraid of me are you? Well, you should be.'

I howl at her. Scream into the spinning sky. Something wild has taken me over. I thought my anger had left me but it's very much alive.

Nothing good comes without work. I have to try to control it. Ten. Nine. Eight.

'Stop.' She's crying.

Seven. Six. Five. 'What do you want from us?'

The sea is so close and it's roaring.

Five. Five. Five. 'Answer me.'

Cold seawater sprays into my face on the shattering wind and I see myself from above as if I am flying over the scene. From above I am the bully. I am the one standing over a small child, shouting and scaring. She's so small. So young. I know her story. I know how it feels when the darkness takes over.

Four. Three. Two. Count. Breathe. I feel cold. The heat has gone from the girl and I can see she is as exhausted as I am. I can't keep this up forever. This all-consuming anger. I have got to stay calm. Reason with her.

One. 'Tell me what you want.'

She carries on crying. I soften my voice as much as I can against the biting wind. 'I'm sorry. Listen. Really I am. I just want to sort this out.'

No response.

'Please.' I'm so very cold suddenly. I'm not sure if I'm crying myself. 'Please.'

She looks up from where she is crouched, and her face is so pitiful. I crouch down so I'm the same height.

'I just want to have a friend.' Sobs make her shoulders heave up and down. 'Why does everyone hate me?'

'I don't hate you.' I'm surprised to find it's true. 'I just don't know what you want from us.'

'Everyone hates me. Even my mother left me.'

This is where the rage comes from. Because she doesn't want to be without her mother. I know this rage. I've felt it myself.

'She didn't leave you. There was a terrible…' I choose my words carefully. I've learned the power of words. How the wrong ones can damage so badly. How the right ones are so important. The bombs that fell on her and her mother were dropped on purpose by people under orders and I don't want to lie. I move closer to her so she can hear me better. 'It was so unfair.'

'What do you mean?'

'When you ran from…' I feel so tired but the

truth is the only way forward. 'When you ran from my Mam-gu, from Olwen, and the other children, where did you go? Can you remember?'

'I hid. Deep in the woods. Until I was certain they had left. Until night fell.' She struggles with the words. 'I went home and there was nothing. A flash of light and heat. And then nothing at all. Just this.'

I take this in and try to think what to say. The wind whips my thoughts from me.

'She left me. My mother. Here on my own.'

She sobs again and I clench my fists. I have to finish this.

'She didn't leave you. Not on purpose.'

'I don't know where she went.'

I clear my throat. 'She died. I'm sorry.'

The girl cries more and I hate myself but I need to put an end to her misery. 'It was the war.'

At the word 'war' I can see her face flooding with memories. It's an awful thing to watch.

'There were planes.' She is frozen in thought.

I am crying now.

'I was running to tell my mother. But I couldn't run fast enough and… Oh no. I don't want to remember again. I don't want to see it all again.'

She covers her eyes with her hands.

I get even closer. 'You are not alone.'

She takes her hands down and looks straight into my eyes. I see it all with her. She is running and not making it in time. I see her anger and despair.

I think of my own anger. The destruction of it. The energy it takes. The way it kills everything in its path.

'I couldn't get to her.'

'You have to forgive yourself.' Whirlwinds of sand gust around us. I'm shouting this to myself and her. 'You can choose to stop this.' Particles of ice sprinkle my face. 'You have to be strong.'

'I don't know how.'

'I don't know how either, but I'm going to try so hard.' I am shouting again because of the blasting wind. It tumbles my words away. 'You need to try hard too.'

I think of the pain that Mam-gu has carried with her. I think of the courage that Mam uses every day to fight her depression. 'We can do this. Together. I will let my anger go but you have to do it too. It's a pact.'

'I don't understand.'

'A pact is a promise between friends. We will have a pact that we will move on. And let our anger go.' The air zings and there is something moving in the corner of my eye. 'We won't use our anger to scare people anymore.'

'We are friends?'

'We are.'

'Pact.'

'Pact.'

There are voices out there carried by the wind. 'I think your mother is calling you.'

'I think yours is calling you.'

'Goodbye.'

'Goodbye, friend.'

The ice particles turn to snowflakes. Thick snow like feathers. Swooping like birds. White and wild and free.

Spring

It's spring half-term and we are back for another holiday. It's now our favourite place. The woods are filled with bluebells, bluey-purple nodding carpets. When the soft warm wind picks up, the cherry blossom scatters like tiny fluffs of floating magic.

I'm strolling down to the beach with Sherlock because he needs a rest from the endless devoted attention of Narnia. He's lazy and hot and his tongue lolls out of the side of his mouth. I pick him up and kiss the side of his face. He reciprocates by licking the inside of my ear. It's gross but in a funny kind of way. Snow has gone ahead with Narnia and her new friend Scarlett from school who's come with us. They were practising their poetry for an assembly performance as they went. I've heard it so many times I know it by heart.

My rucksack is heavy, and I have to keep pausing to get my breath back. Not too much of a chore to have to stop for a rest on this glorious day. When I do I blow a few dandelion clocks and make a few wishes.

I listen to a woodpecker drumming for grubs and pick a piece of Ladies' Smock, remembering Mam-gu's warning never to bring it into the house because it is sacred to the fairy kingdom. Mam-gu always believed there was something else and now I believe it too. I miss her so much but I know she's still here somewhere, and at peace now. I know because now I always trust my instincts and listen to my heart.

Lots of tourists walk their dogs or bicycle along in the amber end of light. Some of them stop to pat Sherlock and say what a beauty he is. I tell them he's the best dog in the world. Narnia is, of course, the second best.

The sea splashes peach sparkles close up and shimmers in orange and fiery gold to the horizon. A cormorant flies low down to the water and a heron dips its beak in the shallows' frills.

I dump my bag and watch oystercatchers scoot the edge of the tide, jackdaws bathing and pecking, guillemots crowding together on the distant cliffs as the sun continues to sink. Charlie and Enfys wave from further down the beach. We donated Erika's doll to the library for their history display. She looks happy there in the middle of all those books. I'm glad she is with friends. Enfys is wearing saffron yellow, topped off with a hat of velvet jay-feather blue. I wave back then point to my boots which she and I decorated with little golden suns. I'm learning new things from her all the time. We keep in touch online.

That strange woman who scared us all that time ago walks past and nods to me. I guess we'll never know what happened to her sister. I smile to show her I'm friendly now.

I'll have to get a move on as I'm meeting the others for the film and everyone will worry if I'm late. We are going to an outdoor cinema screening of *Jaws* further down the beach. The locals invited all the people staying at the caravan site. One of them has even provided a candy-floss machine and I'm looking forward to spinning sugar into a blue, frothy cloud.

It's good here. It's a happy place. Sherlock is lying in a rock pool to cool his belly. I let him stay there. This is probably best done alone anyway. When I get to the edge of the sea I take off my boots and roll my jeans up to my knees before paddling out. The water is surprisingly warm. The sea is starting to take on the thick green colours of night beneath its radiant surface. There's a bit of mist gathering a little way off. I keep my nerve. I don't let my imagination catch me at the corner of my eyes. You could see shapes in the mist if you looked at it the right way. You could imagine that you saw the shape of a girl if you'd been through what I have.

There's hardly anyone at this side of the beach now. Two kids who were happily filling their wellies with water have been scolded by their mam and taken off home in tightly buttoned coats. Sherlock has just spotted Narnia at the far side of the beach so he's raced off. It's so quiet here. The sky is a deep red glow as the sun slides into the sea.

I undo my rucksack. I want to say something special, to say goodbye properly to Mam-gu and to Erika, but I don't know what. So I say a few lines from Snow's school poem as I start to let them all plip, plip, plip into the sea.

One fleeting moment as the sun is setting,
One gentle moment as the night falls fast,
To bring to mind the things that are forgotten,
Now scattered in the dust of ages past.

Like white-foamed waves that break on lonely
beaches,
Like the wind's song where no one hears the
wind…

I can't remember the next line.

I tip the rucksack up and watch our sea glass collection drop into the water, sinking and disappearing as if they are part of a dream. Let all those bits of lives keep tumbling and glowing. Telling their stories and getting more beautiful as time goes by.

Acknowledgments

The Beach Party

Kite flyer, sunny morning smiler, the clear bit at the crest of a wave – Janet Thomas.

Deep sea diver, sandcastle builder, intrepid explorer, ffrind – Ben Illis.

Moonpaths of gold on midnight blue waters, most merry mermaids, singers of seasons, beloved – Mum and Jo.

Drawing patterns in the sand, cariad, rock climber, a flower of the sea, my very favourite cwtcher – Rosie Marina.

Splashing about, sending out ripples, kicking up crystals, wave jumpers – Penny Thomas, Megan Farr, Rebecca Lloyd.

Weaver of morning mists, a sparkling circle enchantress – Anne Glenn.

Fireflies, flitting through the darkness, bright &
beautiful – Rhian Ivory, Sharon Marie Jones,
Jennifer Killick.

Partying properly & flamboyantly in flip-flops –
Team BIA.

At the dawn of an idea, early readers, floating out
paper boats – Lu Hersey, Anna McKerrow, Carly
Holmes, Guy Bass, Sharon Tregenza, Stevie
Davies.

Glittery ghost lover, creative genius,
adventuresome artist, spindrift & smart –
Tamsin Rosewell.

Wisps of magic, memories, clouds, beyond the
line where the land and sea meet – Ruth and
George.

Flotsam collectors, natterers, fellow laughers –
Beth J-P and Jane.

Around the tartan picnic blanket – Lorelei
(Griff) and Beatrice Snow for letting me steal

their names. Kate, Ellen, Lizzie, Rahul, Rosalind, Dhana, Cler and Nicola J.

Radiant rays from a lighthouse – Laura Jones, who named Charlie, and Rachael Rees-Jones who named Gwenllian, both as part of Authors for Grenfell.

Rockpool bather, stone digger, cartographer – Watson Jones, dog.

The dappled mornings, lazy evenings, magical days, owl-filled nights, quickly changing seas and skies – Pembrokeshire.

Keeping me buoyant – Literature Wales, Welsh Books Council.

I've saved the best till last. My readers – you are the points of dazzling light on the ocean, you are the shimmering pieces of sea glass, you are the shifting tides, you make the words float and eddy, you are the stories.